HESITATION WOUNDS

HESITATION WOUNDS

a novel

AMY KOPPELMAN

The Overlook Press
New York, NY

This edition first published in hardcover in the United States in 2015 by
The Overlook Press, Peter Mayer Publishers, Inc.

NEW YORK
141 Wooster Street
New York, NY 10012
www.overlookpress.com
For bulk and special sales, please contact sales@overlookny.com,
or write us at the above address

Library of Congress Cataloging-in-Publication Data

Koppelman, Amy, 1969-
Hesitation wounds / Amy Koppelman.
pages ; cm
I. Title.
PS3611.O675H47 2015   813'.6–dc23   2015024436

Book design and typeformatting by Bernard Schleifer
Manufactured in the United States of America
ISBN US: 978-1-4683-1218-8

FIRST EDITION
2 4 6 8 10 9 7 5 3 1

For Brian, Sammy, and Anna
and for Marie

The park admits the wind,
the petals lift and scatter

like versions of myself I was on the verge
of becoming; and ten years on

and ten blocks down I still can't tell
whether this dispersal resembles

a fist unclenching or waving goodbye. . . .

—from the poem "Sakura Park" by Rachel Wetzsteon

one

This is WHAT I KNOW: THE PEOPLE WHO LOVE YOU LEAVE. But you already know that. We all think we know. Yet somehow . . . at some point we are without. And it's like walking through life without the sky. Flight risk endangers those on land. Still I look for you. Absorbing impact in well-soled shoes. A sidewalk with bicyclists. Don't step on the crack and so on. Betrayal— and that's ultimately what we're talking about here, don't kid yourself—comes in many forms. Yours happened to be un-adorned. Like how concrete when wept upon becomes slippery.

In the middle of the jungle, a boy hears *woo* and releases his hand-carved javelin. The wooden stick lands to cheers. The *woos* and *woo-hoos* diminish into background noise. A quiet din. He thinks this is what the ocean must sound like, which is a rational thought for a boy who's landlocked.

It's only later, four years perhaps, that the boy realizes that there are no waves and he is in fact no longer standing. A javelin driven through the center of his foot has leveled him. Metal besting bone. He tries to escape into the skyless winter night, but the spear anchors. The boy eventually frees himself. His severed foot an afterthought. But you already knew that too. Your laces frayed at the ends.

I was with a girlfriend of mine last night and we were talking about David Foster Wallace. "It's been three years since he killed himself," I said. And she said, "Yep." Waited a beat. "And he's still dead."

A few days before, a woman I know posted a picture of her two children on Facebook. Her husband died in the second tower on their little boy's second day of school. The woman wrote, "Ten years is a long time and no time at all." The boy is tall like his father. The girl has his eyes.

And he's still dead.

This is what I know: The people you love leave. Some, like Dad, are struck by the illogical hand of fate. Others are defeated by time. Only the cruel ones take initiative. You chose a Friday afternoon in September. Robbing me of weekends.

A husband. A child. A life.

There are rats in the city. Giant rats. They roam the streets like rabid dogs. In North Korea, they are hunted and deep-fried. In China, they are marinated and put on the grill. Maybe in another universe they are loved. If I close my eyes and remain still, I can feel you. Sometimes.

Your arm around my shoulder.

They gave Dad six weeks and he made it two years. They gave you a lifetime. A sneak attack. Sure. In a second from now a bomb can detonate. A heart rupture. A skeleton shatter. But, and this took me years to figure out, every effective assault begins as silence.

Fear. Grief. Want.

An ambush can be as gaudy as combustion or as innocuous as the vibration of a cell phone. Which is how it happened to me. This time. On a morning just like any other morning. I had stopped at the Korean grocer around the corner from the hospital when the phone shook. "Hello?"

The voice on the other end said, "Dr. Seliger?" and I answered, "Yes, this is she." And then the voice said, "This is Mike Harrop from One World Adoptions. I have good news." I felt my heart begin to beat. The clip-clop of hope. "I think we found your daughter."

I waited. Over a year. Paperwork. Immigration. And then one morning there I was. Unplugging the toaster. Turning off lights. Locking the door. Making my way down a well-lit street. A yellow cab slowed to a stop. "Kennedy Airport," I said. As we crossed the bridge I took a moment to nod my head in gratitude. A pale pink sky.

Later. In the terminal. I bought a box of Cracker Jack. I mention this because a box of Cracker Jack, in spirit, is essentially what I've come to have faith in after all these years. Twenty-eight years. Deep lines flank the sides of my mouth. Every so often I pluck an unruly hair from my chin. Candy-coated popcorn, peanuts, and a prize. Sure, they've changed too. Long gone are the days of miniature compasses and plastic rings. The free treasures are paper now. That morning the Cracker Jack elves gave me the code to their pinball app. Yes, it's easy to roll your eyes.

Pinball? Smartphone? Really?

Stop.

Belittling nostalgia is a frightened man's parlor trick. Be grateful for any prize. Even a paper fortress, albeit briefly, provides shelter from rain.

And you're still dead.

But I already knew that. So when Jim asked, "Ever hear the one about the archaeologist and the elephant, Dr. Seliger?" I should have replied, "Yes." Except I was thrown by the elephant, so I wavered, "The archaeologist and the elephant?"

"Yeah. The archaeologist and the elephant."

"No, I can't say I have."

"Well, there was this guy . . ." Jim leaned forward in his chair and smiled the way you used to smile when you knew you had a good story for me. "He was a renowned archaeologist, but this story begins before he was renowned. It started when he was in graduate school. He must have been around twenty-five, twenty-six . . ."

I thought, as Jim began telling me the story, that the child that once occupied his broad shoulders and flickering eyes couldn't have foreseen himself as a man. Yes, perhaps ensnaring bad guys, extinguishing fires, leaping from tall buildings in a single bound, but not as he was just then. The night before his last treatment. Blue cloth robe. Sports socks. Daydreams exist without stomach pain and the smell of piss, which is, I guess, a good thing.

"So one day he's tooling around Africa in his Jeep and sees, through binoculars, an elephant struggling in the grass. He drives closer and realizes that the elephant has a branch protruding from its foot, so the archaeologist takes a wrench from the toolbox he kept in the back of his Jeep, walks over to the elephant, and yanks the branch from the elephant's foot.

"Later, when people asked him if he was scared the elephant might trample him, the archaeologist said he hadn't even considered the possibility. It was simply instinct, his wanting to help the elephant.

"That said, there was a moment, the archaeologist confessed, just as he was about to head back to his Jeep there was a moment when he and the elephant connected eyes and for an instant the archaeologist was scared. But instead of stomping him to death, the elephant, eyes beholden, raised his trunk and bellowed. A gesture, the archaeologist was confident, of gratitude.

"Many years later, the archaeologist—by then quite celebrated for his work with iconographic data, ironically—visited one of those faux safaris with his young son. They came across a group of elephants; one fell back and took a step or two in their direction before stopping. The archaeologist thought, from the benevolent look in the elephant's eyes, that this was the same elephant he'd met all those years ago. He said, 'Sonny Boy, this is the elephant I told you about. The one I rescued when I was a student in Africa.' The little boy smiled, opening his eyes as wide as he could in an effort to study the fabled creature. His father said, 'Wait here, okay?'

"The little boy nodded his head up and down. Of course he'd wait there for his dad."

And I thought of you then, when Jim mentioned the little boy, because you did that. You waited. And would have waited there forever if you had to. If it meant Dad would get better and come home. Because that's what a little boy does, right, Dan? A little boy waits for his dad to return, and even when it seems like he may never return, the little boy continues to wait. Because a life without the possibility of return is too much for his little heart to bear. For your little heart. For any little heart, really.

"So the archaeologist, eager to reacquaint himself with his old friend, hopped out of the car and made his way over to the elephant. Sure enough, the elephant lifted his trunk in the same way he had all those years ago, but instead of trumpeting greetings, he wrapped his trunk around the archaeologist, lifted him high into the air, and body-slammed him into the ground.

"And just in case those images alone weren't enough to make an everlasting impression on 'Sonny Boy,' the elephant finished it off by crushing the archaeologist's chest with the same foot the archaeologist had tended to all those years ago." Jim waited a beat. I couldn't tell whether he was trying to gauge my reaction or simply catch his breath.

"The story's standard punch line is, 'Guess it wasn't the same fucking elephant,' but the thing is, I'm not so sure. Why would an archaeologist, a man whose chosen profession is to dig for clues in order to draw a composite of a lost society, allow a single act of kindness to define the character of the African elephant? He could have done this for many reasons,

I guess. Perhaps, while driving through the zoo with his son, he felt a sense of rightness in the world that he associated with his time in Africa and projected that rightness onto the elephant. Or maybe, upon seeing the elephant, he wanted to show his son that decency does, in fact, exist.

"For all we know," Jim went on, "the archaeologist felt guilty for divorcing the boy's mother and wanted to be heroic, or had an undiagnosed brain tumor in his frontal lobe impairing his thinking, or maybe he simply had a death wish. The danger in the clever punch line, Dr. Seliger, in the I-guess-it-wasn't-the-same-fucking-elephant, is that it obscures the story's imperative. Kindness and brutality aren't mutually exclusive. The archaeologist knew this instinctively but it was more important for him to maintain his parable than it was for him to recognize that elephants, like men, are petrified creatures."

The air in the room remained stoic. A halo of fluorescent light hovered above Jim's head. His heel tapped in uniformity with time. Infinity, a postwar high-rise. The frontier, linoleum.

"So which one are you?" I asked. A Freudian prerogative.

"What do you mean?"

"Are you the archaeologist or the elephant?"

Jim sat back in his chair, kicked out his legs, and crossed them at the heels. He, like you, was far too smart to make it easy. "I guess that depends who you ask."

I always asked you. And you always had the answers. Until you didn't. But I asked anyway. Saturday afternoons. I would take the 10:15 train in order to get to you before noon. That first winter I wore your Knicks skullcap and your varsity jacket. That spring your buffalo plaid. Week in. Week out. A stone picnic in suburban air. You probably didn't hear me then. You certainly can't hear me now. Yet I continue. Soundlessly, but with an urgency as remote as it is familiar. I need you to release me, Dan. Before the wave smacks me. Which it will if only because it always has.

I glance over my shoulder hoping to see you. A shadow on the periphery of memory.

Everything you love gets taken away.

It is Jack's death that does it. Man's best friend. Perhaps even more than Dad's. The betrayal in that. To leave your side when you most need him. You can't forgive him, or the world for that matter. For making you believe in them.

Everything you love gets taken away.

I cradle your head on my chest and listen as you repeat it again: "Everything you love gets taken away." And again, "Everything you love gets taken away." Until you surrender onto my folded knees and I watch over you until morning. The tips of my fingers running through your hair.

I can still hear the hum of cars outside your window. The trumpet player on the fourth floor. But I can't hear you whimper. Even now.

Especially now. Perhaps.

Jim got up from the chair and walked over to his hospital bed. So thin now, the samurai's shoulders slanted in such a way that I was immediately reminded of something Dad used to say: "Every object can be reduced to five simple shapes." Jim could be reduced to triangles and squares. He broke the silence: "You know I used to play tennis. Varsity."

"I didn't know that."

"I quit junior year."

"Why?"

"Rebecca Thomas."

"Let me guess; she left you for a football player?"

"Quarterback."

"At least it wasn't the punter."

Jim smiled. "Anyway, a few days later I woke up in a hospital—nude, pink walls, bandaged wrists. I was squatting over a drain in the center of the room, being observed through a peephole by a viewer with a clipboard and what I assume were tidy white nursing shoes. I remember my mom saying, 'Is it that important for you to be liked, Jim?'

"I said—it was visiting hours—'This isn't about being liked, Mother.'

"And she said, 'It is—approval is your mast.' I tried to visualize the parts of the boat: mast, hull, rudder, bow. My toenails were sharp because I'd refused to cut them for weeks. I had come to view my nails as weapons, and it wasn't until right then, as I reached for my foot in an effort to defend myself, that I realized mine had been clipped. At some point in the time between when they brought me in and when I ended up in that room, my fingernails and toenails had been shaped into dull semicircles, benign and inconsequential. It's a funny thing, how conditioned we've become to the magic of the movies: I grieved for what was taken from me without permission, as if fingernails alone are enough to scratch through a cement wall, enough to dig my way to freedom."

"You can play tennis again."

"Not really." Jim slipped off his slipper and tore a piece of dry skin from his heel.

"Why do you say that?"

"Because I'm too old."

"You're forty-six. And you know what they say, forty is the new thirty." Delivering a line like that felt awkward but somehow necessary.

"At my age I'm supposed to take up golf."

"But you wouldn't be starting—you would be restarting."

Jim began to cry then and it still surprised me, the effect of a grown man's tears. I wanted to walk over to the bed and give him a hug. We could stay that way for quite some time, his head on my shoulder, my arms around him. Instead I said, "I played tennis too. I had a mean backhand, double-handed, like Chrissie."

"I'm sure you did." He looked to me for help. "I can't remember anything that's happened in these past two weeks or what you said to me before the six other treatments. Was it the same thing each time—a go-break-your-leg sort of thing, or was it different? All I know is that I lie in bed at night terrified by the prospect of rain."

There was fear in his eyes.

"You are going to be okay," I said. "ECT works."

"Absolutely," he concurred, with numb affect. He didn't believe me.

"It does, Jim. People respond. Sometimes it just takes a little longer."

"'People' brush their teeth, drink coffee, bring sandwiches to work, Dr. Seliger. Cindy brought a ham on toasted white bread to work this morning. Actual people, like my wife, pay mortgages, plan vacations, have kids. I'm not sure what I am or if I am even what would be classified as a human."

"This is the last time and you're done."

"This round."

"You may not need to do it again."

"Do I get a certificate? 'Jim Archer completed his first round of electroconvulsive therapy'?"

I chuckled. "I think I can make that happen."

"Well, in that case, I'll take Cindy out to celebrate. Where do you think we should go? McDonald's seems appropriate, don't you think?"

"Burger King has better fries."

"Oh, so you're a Burger King person." He smiled. "Will I get to wear this gown?"

"Wear a gown where?" Cindy asked as she came into the room. Long live the optimistic girls with shiny eyes and pom-poms. She gave Jim a quick kiss on the lips. "I'm here with provisions. Fried chicken and Dr Pepper."

She turned to me. "You can take the boy out of the South but you can't take the South out of the boy."

"That certainly seems to be the case." I smiled at her.

Camaraderie of sorts. We, those of us who love this breed of man. A collective desperation. Fanning a candle in a hurricane.

"I have a great night planned for us, Jim. We're going to picnic on the bed, watch *America's Got Talent*." She cracked open the Dr Pepper and handed it to him.

Jim took a sip. "They said through thick and thin. They didn't say through *America's Got Talent*."

"They didn't say electric shock either!"

Jim smiled. "I met my match with this one."

"You sure did," I said.

Cindy began unpacking the takeout. "Shoot. They forgot ketchup. I'll swipe some from the cafeteria. Be right back." She hurried out the door.

"Cheerfulness is my wife's default setting. I think that's why I fell in love with her."

"There are worse things to fall in love with, that's for sure." I draped my jacket over my arm, grabbed my briefcase. "If you need anything, just call my cell."

"Will do."

"Tell Cindy that for what it's worth, my money's on the fire eater." I reached for the door.

"Dr. Seliger."

I turned around.

"Don't worry. I'm okay."

And it's not that I forgot that humans believe what they want to believe, what they need to believe in order to survive.

Don't worry. I'm okay.

What I forgot is that I'm human too.

Evan was WAITING FOR ME AT THE ITALIAN RESTAURANT around the corner from our apartment. A table by the window. An average Monday night in autumn. "I'm so sorry . . ." I said as I hurried in.

He took my jacket, pulled out the chair—always a gentleman.

"Thanks, honey. Sorry I'm late. This patient of mine was about to quit."

Evan was focused on the wine list. "Should I get us a bottle?"

I nodded my head.

"Syrah or Bordeaux?"

"Whatever you want."

He waved the waiter over, settled on a Chianti, and returned his attention to me. "I'm sorry, babe, what were you saying?"

Evan's interest in my work had dissipated over the years. My achievements are measured in increments. Days added to someone's calendar, birthday candles, wedding cakes. The outcome isn't necessarily quantifiable, or long lasting, for that matter. A puzzle piece. An electric current. A smile. And so it was hard to blame him. After all, my patients weren't real to him. I was asking him to care about what were essentially characters in a book, and while he did like the movies, he wasn't much of a reader.

"I have this patient who wanted to stop treatment. He's worried he's losing his memory."

"I don't know. That might not be so bad." Evan buttered a slice of bread.

"It might not be so bad? Really? To lose your memory?"

"Yeah. Maybe the guy will be happier." He chuckled to himself.

"Do you mean that?" I asked.

"No. Well, some things. Sure. There are some things I'd be thrilled to forget." He reached across the table and took my hand. "Some people too, but not you."

Menus were given, candles lit, and Evan, a commodities trader who after a recent trip to Rome fancied himself a descendant of the traders of Pompeii, espoused the timeless value of gold. I took it in, charmed by his enthusiasm, his engaged eyes, his familiar smile. The waiter uncorked. Evan poured. And I, unaware of the tempest bubbling from up high, made a toast, the exact words I can't remember, but something like, "I love you, Ev." Yes, something like that, followed by the optimistic clink of our wine glasses. It was then that he told me. His exact words I can't remember, but they were something like "I slept with some waitress when I went to Chicago." Yes, something like that, followed by the sound, the fiery roar, of an erupting volcano. "She's pregnant."

Many people, I suppose now with a bit of distance, respond the same way I did. I raised the glass of wine to my lips in an effort to consume memory: potatoes au gratin, Right Guard deodorant, the tang of his balls. True to form, Evan, after not only fucking but also impregnating another woman, remained erect in his chair. Guilt, I know from professional experience, is rarely detected through posture.

An exotic, perhaps: Asian, Filipina, Indian, the vertical unvaried but the texture of the inner thigh . . . I could have, perhaps, with a few more glasses, bent logic, relegated his behavior to that of a curiosity. Supple. Agile. Young. But Evan, somewhere between sociopath and liar, chose to go for entrapment. "You know how lonely I get in hotels." Men, I know from both professional and personal experience, can be quite adept at playing the victim. "You have to believe me Suze, I never meant to hurt you."

Dad told us with oranges. We were sitting at the kitchen table. It was a weekend morning like any other weekend morning. Mom was making pancakes. Ray was on his way over. Dad reached into a brown bag and handed each of us an orange.

"What are these?"

You were in no mood. "Oranges, Dad."

"And what shape is an orange?"

"It's a circle," I answered.

"Correct. It's a circle but it's round. What is a three-dimensional circle called?"

Neither of us knew.

"A three-dimensional circle is called a sphere. Okay, now raise the orange above your head."

We raised it above our heads.

"What shape is it?"

"It's a sphere," I answered.

"Great. Now move it down and to the right. Three o'clock."

We moved it down and to the right. Three o'clock.

"What shape is it here?"

"Still a sphere," we said.

"So no matter where you move the orange, it's a three-dimensional circle?"

We nodded our heads. "A sphere."

Dad reached into his bag and pulled out a grapefruit. "Okay, what's this?"

You and I kinda looked at each other like *What in the world is he doing?*

"It's a grapefruit," I said.

"And what shape is it?"

"Dad!" I said.

"It's a sphere," you said.

"You willing to put money on it, Daniel?"

"Dad, what's your point?"

The doorbell rang, "I'll get it." I hurried to the door, opened it.

"Hey Susa."

Mom was ladling pancake batter onto the frying pan, "Take a seat, Honey. These will be ready in a minute. I didn't want them to get cold."

Dad tossed Ray an orange. "What shape is that?"

Ray smirked at you. "What shape is the orange?" He rotated it in the palm of his hand for effect. "It's a sphere, Mr. Seliger."

He sat down next to you and Mom presented him with a huge plate of pancakes, "Thanks, Mrs. Seliger. These look amazing."

"Kiss Ass," you said under your breath and we all laughed.

Dad reached back into his bag. "And what shape is this?" He held up the grapefruit.

"A larger sphere?"

Dad, a magic enthusiast, made an abracadabra gesture with his napkin, "Tada." He turned the grapefruit and what appeared to be a whole grapefruit was actually half.

"So what's this a lesson about, guys?" Dad put his silverware down and looked at us. "Any ideas?"

"How something can look different from different angles?"

"Sure, it's about perspective. That's part of it, Suze."

"Because we held the oranges in our hands," Ray said. "So we guessed that the grapefruit was whole too."

"Precedent. That's part of it also."

I glanced at you and you had this kinda haunted look on

your face. It was clear that you'd figured out something that Ray and I had missed. But you didn't announce it. Mom brought over a fresh pot of coffee. Dad began fingering through the paper and nothing. You just sat there looking super sad until you finally said, "It's about certainty."

Dad's eyes began to fill with tears. "Yes, son, it's about certainty."

Three months later, while undergoing experimental brain surgery, Dad died. The surgeon spoke to us personally, still in scrubs. He said he was so sorry. That he knew how much Dad wanted to live and how much he had to live for. He said Dad was brave because he understood the risks of this new procedure but was willing to try anything that might help him survive. He said that once they opened Dad up, though, they knew it was futile. The tumor was simply too big, "It was tantamount to having a small orange lodged in the middle of his brain."

"A sphere," you said under your breath.

I took your hand. "A sphere."

I don't remember what happened when Evan and I walked back to our loft, if I took a bath or shower, how we decided to sleep in the same bed, say goodnight. I do remember, though, the sound of Evan's breath. Steady and even. In, then out. I watched his chest rise and fall. Sleep like death predisposed to mercy. How defenseless we are to the people whose bed we share.

In the morning, I felt Evan tapping my shoulder. "Time to wake up, Suze." I opened my eyes and there was a moment —a split second, the sun streaming through the curtain— before I remembered. Evan handed me a coffee—"I made it just the way you like, a hint of milk, three teaspoons of sugar"—and waited to be acknowledged. I realized then, when he took pride in this, in knowing that I like just a hint of milk in my coffee, that it was over. But instead of saying "It's over" or "Fuck you" or merely asking for the paper, I sat up in bed and said, "How do you know it's yours?"

Bewildered, all he could think to say was, "Why would she lie?"

I began to laugh. Really? Why would she lie, would anyone lie? Why does anyone? And yet this I knew and had known for quite some time: dishonesty refracted through tears is consolation to a woman like me—Evan crept closer, "You said you didn't care about having kids"—a woman who never considered happiness to be a possibility or love a desire.

"Come on, Evan. Over the past couple of years almost everyone we know has had a kid. We've both seen the pleasure it's brought to their lives, but you didn't want one, so . . ."

"I still don't want a kid and I'm not having one."

I tapped the saucer with my spoon, gazed out the window. For it to be effective, I needed to be at least four floors higher. "I know you believe that you aren't having a baby, but you are, Evan. You are having a baby."

Dry, barren, too old to toy with regret, I steadied my voice. Theatrics, after all, are for amateurs. Even so, I couldn't help myself. "If you were going to give someone a baby, shouldn't I have been the one you gave a baby to?"

"I'm so sorry, Suze. I wish you could know how sorry I am. I love you with all my heart. What I had with her was nothing."

"What you had with her?"

"It was nothing, Suze. She was nothing."

"But you didn't use protection."

"She said she was on the pill."

"Jesus, Evan. You have no idea what diseases she has. You're surely not the first customer she's fucked, and then you came home and fucked me and worse slept next to me for weeks and weeks knowing this . . ."

Head bowed, Evan walked over to the window, looked out onto a brick courtyard. "Let's have a baby. Me and you. Let's have a little family." He turned to face me. "I'm ready. Anything. You want to get married? Want to move to a house? Anything you want me to do I'll do. Just don't give up on me, Suze. Please. I love you. I'm just flawed."

In all the years we'd been together, that was the closest he'd ever come to introspection.

"It's too late, Evan."

He knelt before my side of the bed, took my hands in his own. "No, it isn't. We'll go to the most cutting-edge doctor. You'll get in-vitro. Fifty-year-old women have babies these days. You have lots of time."

I threw up then. All over our bedspread. I wiped my mouth with my pajama sleeve and threw up a second time.

On the way to work, I stopped by the market to buy a bottle of water. A little boy perched in the basket of a supermarket cart was eating grapes. His mother told him to chew carefully, "Chew carefully, Billy." Billy's matchbox car, which he had been holding in the palm of his grape-free hand, fell to the floor. I bent over to pick it up and returned the car, a red Corvette, to the boy. "Billy, thank the lady for picking up your car."

"Tank you," the little boy said.

Our eyes met and held. Then he looked away.

They continued down the aisles: a box of macaroni elbows, a bag of chips, a pint of chocolate milk. Their conversation revolved around what would come next. "We are going to pay," the mother said, "then walk home."

The little boy listened attentively. There was lunch ("turkey and cheese") and soccer ("Yes, the kicking game") followed by another nap ("Of course we'll watch *Sesame Street*"). I plucked a box of sugary cereal from a shelf. A bag of pretzels from another. How easy it was to pretend that I too inhabited a world populated with matchbox cars, soccer balls, and grapes.

There we are. See us laughing. My boy is snuggled in the groove of my arm and we are reading a book. I am reading him a book about a crocodile that pilots a spaceship. How silly. Crocodiles aren't astronauts. We are sharing chocolate pudding now. The spoon is the spaceship, I'm the crocodile, his mouth is space. I fly a spoon between his lips . . .

Wee.

And sure, I could see the end. He'd get bigger and learn to feed himself and eventually leave me, but I would have had that. A son. I would be a woman with a son. A mother of a son.

My reflection reproached me in the freezer section. Yes, I answered my replicate self. I might have frozen my eggs. I should have done that. But I didn't. I chose, instead, to let time seal my fate. It was enough to watch from a distance. A boy in a karate gi. A girl in soccer cleats. I told myself I wanted a different life and most of the time I kept busy enough to believe it. But every so often there would be a moment—at the supermarket, let's say, when a little boy drops his matchbox car—*Thank the lady. Tank you*—when I allowed myself to articulate the truth. I've lived my whole life in reaction, Dan. Fear of intimacy masquerading as self-reliance. Inflexibility as conviction. Audacity as fearlessness. To the world, a broken person can appear whole when in truth each action is as automatic and hollow as the knee jerking after being hit with a doctor's hammer.

Jim appeared whole, lounging on a cot, curtain drawn, blue cloth robe. It was still quite early in the morning. If you didn't know any better, you might think he was a guy scheduled for an appendectomy. But not in that waiting area. The fifth floor is for affairs of the brain. In the next compartment, a toddler in footie pajamas sat on his mother's lap. Bandaged skull. Hollowed eyes. Even if the tumor turns out to be benign, he had faced this, the scrutiny of mortality's gaze. Three years old. Forfeiture's radiance rushed between the crib's metal bars, branding him. The mother held him tight. Death. Inescapable. Sat next to her. Laughing.

And this is where I concede. Modern medicine, even with its abilities to stabilize mood, improve sleep, and focus concentration, ultimately provides little fortification against memory, which can, on any given day, at any given time, penetrate a fortress of pills. Because, in truth, we spend our lives trying to hold on to memory, clutching it in the palm of our hand like a kid holds on to a fistful of Cheerios, which, over time, an afternoon at the park for instance, will mutate into a gooey glob nearly unrecognizable to anyone other than the mother of this toddler.

But the kid will hold on to them, because, at the very least, they are *his* Cheerios, and by virtue of their existence in his hand, he is alive, a little boy in the park with a fistful of Cheerios. It's only when he sees a fellow boy at the base of the slide lift a perfectly whole Cheerio to his mouth does the kid become aware his are damaged. It is only then that he begins to mourn.

What I know now and didn't know then or knew but didn't allow myself to accept, is both boys, Bandaged Head and Fistful of Cheerios, all three, actually—Bandaged Head, Fistful of Cheerios, Jim—all three will spend the rest of their lives pinpointing moments of defeat. They will analyze incidents, play out every "if only." If only he hadn't had a brain tumor as a child. If only he hadn't clasped his hand so tight. If only he hadn't changed medication.

In addition to the affliction of memory, or perhaps because of it, I had once again been forced to accept the reality that one's power of denial, perhaps as much as treatment, determines prognosis. A year and a half ago I would have acknowledged, but mitigated, the mental component of the disease. I would have stuck with science: neurotransmitters, the limbic system, electrode placement. But then Jim Archer came through my office door and all the years of subjugated thought and reflexive denial conflated. The past and the present began to complicate one another. I was a sixteen-year-old girl again. Jim was my brother.

And it's not that I haven't thought about you, Daniel. A day hasn't passed in the last twenty-eight years that I haven't felt your presence or heard your voice or reached for the phone to call you. But for some reason, from the moment Jim walked into my office, I was overcome with an urgency as remote as it was familiar. I'm not sure if it was Jim's build, the timbre in his voice, or the fact that he came in wearing a Zeppelin T-shirt. Maybe it was just timing. Maybe I was finally ready to face all that I had skillfully avoided. Whatever it was, I had to save Jim Archer. Persuade him to carry forward. To allow himself, at the very minimum, the option of growing old.

I glanced at the book Jim had with him. "You're reading Hitchens?"

"Yep."

"What side are you on? God or No God?"

"I wouldn't mind seeing that all-star band people talk about."

"Me too."

"Yeah, but what you'd want and what I'd want in a concert are two different things."

"How do you know that?"

"You'd probably want a narrative of some sort—a show, you know what I mean, with a beginning, middle and end? Even a theme would be fine with you. Rock. Pop. Country." Jim thought of something and chuckled to himself, "Disco! How groovy would that be. He's got practically all the Gibb brothers up there at this point."

"Sounds fab." I smiled.

"Totally. But you see I'd want something different. I'd be in it for the atmosphere. All that Kumbaya shit. I mean how great would that be. *Hear me crying my Lord, kum bay ya.* Imagine Sam Cook and Joplin harmonizing? *Hear me praying my Lord, kum bay ya.* Hendrix on the guitar. Yeah, if there's a heaven I'd want to spend my days hanging on the mound, smoking fatties, watching the poor miserable versions of ourselves roaming the earth ruminating the God question."

"Do you think life would be easier for you if you knew the answer to what happens next?"

"*Hear me singing my Lord, kum bay ya.* I can't sing for shit." Jim laughed. "Yeah—of course. Imagine what it would be like to live life free of the fear of death."

"Pretty nice, I suppose."

"Let's say heaven is real—an afterlife that rivals the movies—but the catch is when you die, assuming you go to heaven, you can only hang out with one person from your past life. Who would you want to see?"

I tried to deflect, "You mean who would I want to go disco dancing with?"

"Sure. Disco dancing. Parachuting. Who would you want to see again?"

"I don't know."

"Of course you know."

"But this isn't about me."

"Come on, Dr. Seliger. I let you fry my fucking brain. Tell me, if you could spend time with any one person again, who would you want to see?"

Patients, no MATTER WHAT THEY EXPRESS OVER A CUP OF coffee with friends or how many times they ask me how my weekend was, want their shrink to be well dressed and professional. They don't want to know (not really) anything about me. And they aren't supposed to. The role of the patient is to be the sole character in a narrative of one. So I greet both the new ("Hello, I'm Dr. Seliger") and the returning ("Nice to see you again") with a practiced but sincere smile.

My work appearance—blouse, slacks, loafers—is neutral rather than genderless. My office is clean. Diplomas, in coordinating black frames, hang on one wall. A bookshelf with psychiatry journals and reference books occupies another. A freestanding scale, blood pressure monitor, and a classic five-part brain model are the only evidence that mine is, in fact, a practicing doctor's office.

I specialize in the treatment of treatment-resistant depression. When the MAOIs, TCAs, TeCAs, SNRIs, and SSRIs fail to get results, the patients are sent to me. And I zap 'em. Or that's what the movies would have you think. Electroconvulsive therapy (ECT), or, as it's better known, shock treatment, is only shocking in that it doesn't actually cause much, if any, physical pain. A patient's emotional pain is an entirely different story.

I sit in a high-backed ergonomic leather office chair behind a formidable walnut desk. On top of the desk sits a phone, a prescription pad, and a can of Diet Coke. Two hardback chairs, neither of which is particularly comfortable, face the desk. No flowers or photographs, but a box of tissues is within easy reach.

There are inherent implications in my choice of presentation: efficiency is obtainable through orderliness, success through proper conduct, professional distance through protocol. Patients do not come to me to meander in thought, transfer emotion, unearth secrecy. Complex stories about childhood and innuendo are not routine. I take the past into account, sure, but keep the conversation straightforward: name, date of birth, symptoms. A brief and fact-driven family history leads to a few questions about the patient's general health and well-being.

Finally, I catalog any and all medications being taken, in order to avoid contraindication. This is not to say I hurry my patients through. I make clear my willingness—more than willingness—to discuss the mechanics of the brain, titrate medication, confer with a patient's ob-gyn, psychologist, social worker, guidance counselor, psychoanalyst, or clergy person. I explain the possible side effects, suggest strategies to mitigate them, elucidate the biological and genetic components of mental disorders. I'll even happily consider the benefits of augmenting Western medicine with Eastern philosophies.

But I don't, at least I didn't, do talk therapy. Up until Jim became my patient, I did everything in my power not to console. I left that to those professionals who specialize in the field of empathy. I was primarily a scientist. I provided a medical solution to illnesses that present as emotional problems. Hence, the hardback as opposed to upholstered chairs. A patient should feel within a comfort zone but not quite comfortable. I didn't, as you know more than anyone, start out this way. Wouldn't you say, Dan, that I had, as a child, an almost precocious ability to love? But life has ways of throwing even the most dedicated member of The Baby Doll Club of America off course.

I had, I thought at the time Jim came to see me, finally regained my footing. Mom had recently died, and although her death had been expected, it was still devastating. The machinations—ceremony, procession, cemetery. The stark fact that living too long means nearly all your friends and colleagues, those that would have attended, honored, eulogized you, are dead. But even that in the end was manageable. As were the meetings with the building manager and tag sale ladies. It startled me, actually, the ease with which I was able to undertake and complete these tasks. There is an entire industry hell-bent on accommodating the bereaved. In less than one week I had sorted through Mom's life. Clothing, photographs, letters . . .

I keep her green ceramic vase on my kitchen table now. Every week I fill it with yellow flowers just as she did. Freesias, tulips, buttercups, depending on the season. A few other valuable pieces went to a consignment store on Eighth Street. Every few months a check arrives: $22 for a crystal ashtray, $80 for a lamp, $145 for a pair of gold earrings. All bought by those seeking the allure of history, without knowledge of the past. The alternative, it seems, to preserving and/or purchasing memory is to simply discard it. But this, like so many things in life, is easier said than done, because once it's discarded, once there's no one left that remembers— the night you ran around the fountain, the cold stone against your feet, the song that was playing on the radio—once there's no one left that remembers, it's as if it never happened.

Mom kept your bedroom door closed. I didn't press her about it because I understood. With the door shut, anything was possible. You were away for the weekend, studying for a chemistry exam, taking a nap. But when the door was open, you were nothing but dead. Then out of the blue one night she said, "Suze, if it's okay with you I'd like to paint Daniel's room mauve."

"Mauve?" I asked.

"Yeah" she said, "I've been thinking about it for a long time and I'd like it to be mauve."

Mom turned your room into a sanctuary of sorts. She bought a new turntable, a soft carpet, a slew of altar candles. It seemed absurd to me, as if some combination of meditation and ambient sound could somehow fill the loss in the spaces between. But it did. Mom spent hours upon hours in that room. Exposure to pain limited to the parameters of memory. A safe room, where life exists only on replay and there are no surprises.

So, other than your bedroom, when Mom died our apartment was basically as you would remember it. Black leather sofa, glass top kitchen table, hanging ferns. Mom finally, thank goodness, replaced those seafoam green sheets she had stapled to her bedroom window with real curtains but my room hadn't changed at all. Winnie was still resting against my pillow. Some concert T-shirts and a Bedazzler were in the top drawer of my dresser. A pair of old Frye boots and a couple of sweaters in the closet. Your Bernard King poster hung on my door. Your subway map above my bed. The plastic stars you put on my ceiling were still there. Most of them anyway.

When I walked out the door of our apartment for the last time I didn't allow myself to look back. Instead I marched forward, with nothing but a single green vase and a large cardboard box between my arms.

The box was smaller than I remembered. Certainly smaller than it should be—as if everything that mattered—everything that made you you—could fit into a box of any size. At the time though, I remember thinking, "If a stranger opens this box two hundred years from now, she will know who my brother was." A naive supposition for many reasons. Chiefly because all that there was in the box was what I put in it.

I'd probably put different things in it now. Or I wouldn't. Maybe I'd remember you just the same no matter what additional knickknacks I bubble-wrapped. Locked away, memory is easy to preserve as truth. The thing is, what you choose to forget is as important as what you allow yourself to remember. But I didn't know that. I thought I was saving everything I needed Dan but I was really only saving what I could bear.

I kept your Evel Knievel action figure. I kept the motorcycle and the launch pad and that hideous purple sweatshirt you loved. I was hesitant to take it out of the plastic. So many years later and yet I was scared that if I smelled you, I'd start to cry and not be able to stop. But instead as I pressed my face against it I heard you say, "You ready, Suze?" Your voice immediate and alive.

It's a cold day. A very cold day. January maybe. I am young. You're a bit older but you're also young. And yet there you are, a purple hoodie and jeans. There you are, leading me to the center of the ice. "I got you," you say. Your eyes blue.

Mom is standing at the edge of a pond. She is shouting at us to be careful. Shouting at you to "hold on tight, Daniel. Make sure she doesn't fall."

"I promise," you holler back. And you didn't. You never let me fall.

But I let you fall, Dan.

I let you fall.

Come on, Dr. Seliger. I let you fry my fucking brain. Tell me, if you could spend time with any one person again, who would you want to see?

Jim was waiting for an answer. And it wasn't too much to ask, was it? That I surrender something to him, something in exchange.

"If I could see anyone, I'd want to see my brother."

And so the walls within me crumbled, which often occurs when matter and faith collide. A rocket booster and salt water. I laugh now thinking about it. How I clutched time. A woven braid of straw can ignite from the mere flicker of memory's flame. Yet there I am. Swinging from the rafters. A novice on the flying trapeze. Even so, I beguiled. Gravity momentarily an illusion.

Daniel Seliger leaves behind a sixteen-year-old sister: Susanna Rose (in memory of her fraternal grandmother) Seliger. The five-foot-six high school junior is an above average but not particularly exceptional student. An alternate on the volleyball team, she has lean, muscular legs that look particularly great in the requisite spandex.

Suza (pronounced Suza by friends and family) wouldn't agree with this assessment. Her upper arms, for instance, although toned, appear (only to her, perhaps) to be bulky. This is easily remedied with long-sleeve, off-the-shoulder shirts, which fortunately happen to be in style.

Suza's also self-conscious about her stomach. According to

Christopher Davies (a young man who continued well into his teens to dig for gold in public) Suza has a "pop belly." This astute observation gleaned during the fourth-grade rendition of The Sound of Music.

Suza, a tree, was costumed in a green leotard and tights. Christopher, not a participant in the musical, conveyed his insight from the second row of the school auditorium. He did this the only way a nine-year-old-boy-with-a-crush-on-an-oak-tree can. There was, needless to say, much giggling and finger pointing.

The deceased, also in attendance, took it upon himself to visit Mr. Davies after the final curtain. No words were exchanged. He simply punched the boy square in the face. Then, uniquely aware of consequence, the deceased walked straight to the principal's office and turned himself in. Suza waited just outside the classroom door every day after school for the two weeks her brother was sentenced to detention.

Christopher apologized to Suza (he wasn't allowed Atari for a month) and subsequently (four years later) asked her to the movies (ET) which she politely (but with great satisfaction) declined. Even so, the residual of the pop belly comment remains, accounting for her gratuitously loose-fitting tops.

Suza's is a slow beauty: a heart-shaped face, straight nose, full lips. Her skin is quite pale, milky almost. Her long hair straight and brown. Her eyes in the pure aesthetic sense aren't particularly special. Oval, nicely spaced, a slightly deeper brown than her hair.

Yet if Suza were to look at you, to actually allow you to make eye contact, she'd impart a reflective understanding, a well of com-

passion, a poignant beauty restricted to children who witness death. And twice now. First her father. Now her brother.

"There's only so much one young girl can take," she overheard her friend Jennifer's mom say to their school guidance counselor. Mr. Attenbury, hyper-aware of his surroundings, saw Suza approaching and in an effort to distance himself from the comment said, "You'd be surprised. Girls are quite resilient by nature." But even then, Suza knew this wasn't true. Resiliency isn't a characteristic predetermined by gender. Resiliency, like a cartwheel, requires core strength and a disregard for gravity. Only one of which can be willed.

Daniel Seliger leaves behind his sixteen-year-old sister Susanna Rose (in memory of her fraternal grandmother) Seliger. Suza is a Capricorn, a Knots Landing *fan, and a virgin. More Benatar than Blondie (although she's partial to feather earrings and big hair), she is and isn't any one of a hundred girls. There she goes, making her way home from school. One foot in front of the other.*

"Shit. I'm so sorry," Jim said.

"Don't be. Really. It happened a long time ago," I said.

"Yeah, but it wasn't my place to ask."

"No, it's fair. You trust me to 'fry your brain' as you so delicately put it. I think that earns you the right to know a little about me."

And then, because stating the obvious is often an act of self-preservation, I checked my watch and said, "They should be here soon."

"Then excuse me for a moment." Jim stood and walked

down the hall to the bathroom. Watching him, I thought, he lumbers like a toddler. I visualized his mother, knees bent, arms open, "Come to me." There was Jim, four years old, exchanging balance: right foot to left.

And there I am. Not much older than Jim. Six maybe. There I am standing watch from my apartment window, waiting for the sequence of lights to change. You, no longer a boy free to cry, linger at the corner across the street from our apartment building. You're holding a brown paper bag from the deli in one hand and your Walkman in the other. You're also waiting for the lights to change, and when they do, you begin crossing the street. What a burden for you to have had at such a young age: being responsible for my loneliness.

I thought then, as I had thought many times before, that it's all really about loneliness. The inevitability of our aloneness. Six feet under. Velvet rope. Satin lining. We start alone. We end alone. We are alone as we are pushed down the hallway. We are alone as electrodes get attached to our skull by well-meaning explorers. We are alone as currents instigate a grand mal seizure. A foam block between teeth. Hands bound. We are alone at our last breath, even when being held. We are always alone.

Jim came back from the bathroom. "Jeez, that's some look on your face. I'm really sorry, talking about your brother must have upset you." He leaned against the edge of the hospital bed.

"To tell you the truth, I wasn't thinking about him. I was thinking about a conversation I had with Ken Kesey."

"Really? What were you two chatting about?"

"I was telling him that electroconvulsive therapy is entirely different now."

"And what did Mr. Kesey have to say?"

"He said, 'You're asking me to make a concession I'm not ready to make.'"

"And you said?"

"I said, 'You can do it, Kenny. It's all an issue of desire.' And he rolled his eyes and said, 'But why would I ever do that? Don't you like seeing Jack in the front row of Laker games?'"

Jim was thoroughly entertained. "Really, Mr. Kesey said that?"

"Yes." I smiled. "I told him I really don't care about Jack. I said, 'Kenny, I overcame my daddy issues a long time ago and quite frankly, I'm a Knicks fan.'"

"He must have scoffed at you. Mr. Kesey."

"Of course he did, but laughter at another's expense is easy."

"What kind of laughter is hard?"

This took me a minute. I wanted to say something meaningful, something about the quality of laughter, earned laughter versus received laughter, but all I could think to say was, "To laugh in spite of, I guess."

Jim looked back out the window. It was a beautiful autumn day, the leaves were changing color, the air cooling. Without turning away, Jim said, "Can you tell me a story?"

"What type of story?"

"Tell me what six years from now looks like for me."

I smiled, but only slightly. "Six years?"

Jim nodded.

"Okay." It took a second to formulate my thoughts. Jim wanted a guarantee more than a story. A clairvoyant with a law degree. A parachuting notary. A cucumber in a pickle pot. I clasped my hands. Sat up in my chair. Took a breath and began.

"Six years from now, you will have a little boy named Simon, which will seem like an odd choice that you should name your child Simon, but that is what you will do. Six years from now, you and Cindy will have a four-year-old son named Simon and you will stay up at night watching him breathe in, then out, and most mornings, certainly every morning he doesn't have preschool, you will lift him onto your shoulders and walk down the street, to the coffee shop on the corner. You will enter, say hello to everyone, make your way to your table, the one all the way in the back just outside the kitchen. You will have an espresso and toast and your boy will have a chocolate chip cookie that's the size of his face.

"When you get home, Cindy will say, 'Not again, Jim! You didn't—a chocolate chip cookie for breakfast?' And you'll say, 'Simon said.' And you and Simon will laugh a laugh exclusive to fathers and sons. You will giggle in unison. Co-conspirators: the masters of chocolate chip cookies and water guns and purple dinosaurs that talk. You will check your watch, hand him over to Cindy, and go to work on some article or something, and you will look out the window and see them digging, a little boy and his mom planting bulbs. You will focus on your computer screen, then out again toward the short path that leads to your front door, and you will be happy. You will be happy and grateful that you kept going, and these treatments will seem like a lifetime ago, because they will be a lifetime ago.

"At noon, you will break for lunch, grilled cheese sandwiches, and you will play a game. You will say, 'Lift the corner of your sandwich and make a wish.' Simon will grow up this way—year in, year out—with every sandwich he will peek inside and make a wish. Your wish will always be the same: for this to continue—this kind of happiness. Later, after another few hours at work, the two of you will walk to the park, where he will do the things little boys do at the park. He will run after other children, play in the sandbox, slide. You two will seesaw—you in the center, him at the end, so that the weight is balanced and you are in control of his ups and downs.

"He is learning his letters: 'Yes,' you will say when he points, 'that's a letter "m." What starts with the letter "m"?' And he'll say, 'Mommy,' and you'll say, 'Yes, Mommy!' and hold him, squeeze him against your chest—this boy, your life.

"Yes. It will all be scary. There will be skinned knees, sore throats, and fevers. You will be scared. There will be months that you are running a little short and you'll worry about how you are going to keep this all going, but just then you'll get an email from the editor of *Esquire* asking you to cover the Democratic National Convention. You won't be happy leaving Cindy and Simon, leaving your little house, the clay pots filled with cheerful yellow pansies, the T-ball set on the lawn. As you begin walking down the short front path to the waiting taxicab, he'll call after you, 'Simon says touch your nose.'"

You'll touch your nose.

"'Simon says touch your knees.'"

You'll touch your knees.

"'Simon says have a good trip, Daddy.'" You will put down your bag, walk over to your son, hug him goodbye for a second time. You will remember these treatments like a cancer survivor looks back on chemo. But the present. This boy. His face, his hands, his smile, his arms wrapped around your shoulders, will be what you're thinking about as your plane heads to Colorado.

"Several months later, another morning, another trip to the coffee shop, you will stop by a magazine store and buy a copy of the March issue of *Esquire*. The one your article is featured in—the one that has your name on the cover—and you will say, 'What does that say?' and Simon—with your help—will sound out the letters that make up your name.

"'Dames Archer.'"

"'And what's your name, buddy?'"

And Simon will smile from a bond he will never quite be able to articulate until, well, until maybe he grows up and has a son. 'My name is Pimon Archer!'

"Later, as he carries the magazine, with two hands, into the coffee shop, Simon will say, 'I love you, Daddy,' and at that moment you will remember from where you came and you will be grateful that you made it through all this—that you found a way to survive. You will look at the little guy sitting across the table from you. You will note the smell of coffee beans.

"As you are doing this, your boy will pass you a piece of his chocolate chip cookie and you will hold it on your tongue, its sweetness slowly dissolving into your mouth, and you will think, 'I am happy,' and tears may fill your eyes, but don't worry, it's normal for tears to fill the eyes of those who are happy. You'll wrap your arm around your boy's shoulder and flip the paper over and he'll snuggle into the groove of your arm and listen as you read from the sports section.

"'Tonight is the opening game for the Chicago Bulls. Not since number 23 laced 'em up for the Bulls have fans let themselves feel this optimistic at the start of a season.'

"And Simon will say, 'Who is number 23, Daddy?' You will fold the paper, clasp your hands, and look at him very seriously, and you will say, 'Michael Jordan, son, was the greatest basketball player of all time.' And Simon will sit up straight, his ears peaked, and you will say, 'Michael Jordan played a different game than anyone else before or after him.'

"And so it will begin, your ongoing conversation about the meaning of sportsmanship, courage, loyalty to team. At that moment, you will glance back at the you, as you are now, with your back to the window, wearing that flimsy blue robe, and you will stand at attention and salute yourself, all of this as you continue your conversation with your son: 'The difference between great players and superstars is what they do in the last three minutes. You always want the ball in MJ's hands in the last three minutes. Because when Michael Jordan needed to, he could fly.'"

I stopped. "That's what I see for you six years from now."

There was a knock at the door. An orderly entered with a stretcher. Jim turned from the window. "I hope they let me remember that."

"If they don't, I'll tell it to you again."

Jim rested his head on the pillow. "Do me a favor, make it an oatmeal cookie the next time." And then he turned his attention to the orderly. "Let's do it."

And so the masked man capitulates. Rage before a rising moon.

Little incandescent STARS DANCED ON THE CEILING, promising to defy gravity and stick, which they did for many years until one by one they peeled away and I could no longer remember if they were there at all or if I was only pretending, now habit, to bathe in starlight. I sank into the mattress of our double bed. If stars can push through a stucco sky, then this might be enough, I supposed. Evan wiped my tears with his right thumb. With his left hand, he ran his fingers through my hair. We didn't talk, we just stayed this way for a while. Long enough for me to stop crying and him to feel absolved.

But a glass window is false protection from a parade. Madison Avenue. The southwest corner of Sixty-fifth. Angry at her anonymity yet translucent and bedecked, a mannequin in a chartreuse evening gown stands in the window of Valentino. Evan asked, taking this dummy's hand, if I would like to dance. I looked away, which he, like many men, both flesh and plastic, took for a yes. So he pressed against me, flesh to flesh, beating hearts and I met him because I ought to. After all, I was forty-four, men my age were no longer easy to come by. And "He's a good man," Mom said, after the first and every subsequent time he strayed. Mom, may she rest in peace, possessed many traits both feminine and maternal. An instinct for people wasn't one of them.

What's the saying, Dan? Fool me once shame on you, fool me twice shame on me? It was shame on Evan when he hooked up with an old girlfriend early into our relationship. But after that it was shame on me. Summer intern, shame on me. Yoga instructor, shame on me. Every stripper at every bachelor party he went to, shame on me.

But the thing is, as crazy as it sounds, Evan's transgressions anchored me. I welcomed the pain. The week or two of despair that lead to a night of great sex and subsequent reconciliation. In fact, if I'm being honest, I was complicit in the cycle, turned the proverbial blind eye, suspicion the key to vigilance.

But a baby . . .

Evan somehow assumed that I was enjoying myself and bit me on the other side of my neck. Vampire features were all the rage, and I too can bleed.

Past. Present. Future.

Down the street and around the corner an orchestra of tin men banged their kettledrums as a swarm of bees ascended my pussy. A version of joy. At that moment I recognized that I could no longer pretend—not the stars—not his hand upon mine—not your gravestone or the tugboats on the Hudson or the purple sweatshirt in the garbage bag. I could no longer pretend they were arbitrary. Random is not truth.

Nothing is random.

There is no escape.

Although the book in the bathroom, just to the right of the toilet, begged to differ. "Everyone has cancer cells but everyone doesn't get cancer." Deterrence, an alternative strategy—blueberries and celery sticks—is contingent on the notion of measure. I pictured the brown metronome my piano teacher would rest just above the white keys—throbbing and constant—and how my fingers, unlike my teacher's, could never quite keep up and how similar it felt, as Evan came, finished before I even began.

Later, because routine is comforting, *The Daily Show with Jon Stewart*, I said, "Ginny is having people over on Friday to watch the World Series." An escape hatch, the din of scripted banter filling the space between us. This was a conversation Evan and I had had before, his being a Yankee fan and all. My eyes feigned presence—"I said we'd bring dessert"—as my mind floated. Regret a treacherous air space through which to navigate.

In a little less than a month some waitress in Chicago would have Evan's baby. I wondered what it might be, a boy or a girl? I asked this out loud, always a toe dipper, and he answered with "Boy or girl, it will mean nothing to me. I told you. I won't ever meet it."

I ran my mind through the new delivery systems: text, Twitter, Facebook, email. "You're telling me that one day this woman sends you an email with 'Your Son' as the subject line and you're going to press Delete?"

"Yes," he said, believing this to be true.

"What if the subject line reads 'Shortstop'?"

I should have left. That's what people do. They acknowledge betrayal by walking out the door. Or I should have thrown him out. I should have taken an action of some sort, but instead I said, "Do you love me?"

Evan rolled over, pulled me close. "Of course I love you, Suze."

I could feel his heart beating against my back. *Thump-thump*. He was alive. *Thump-thump*. He was with me in our bed. *Thump-thump*. But that was all I could be certain of. That's all a heartbeat is really, a baseline.

"Why?" I asked.

"Why?"

Thought, though, is an elusive fucker. Imperceptive even to itself at times.

"Why do you love me?"

Thump-thump. It was at this moment. *Thump-thump*. The extra beat between my asking and his answering, when I finally understood. Truth is a fool's imperative. Which is why I found Evan's answer particularly entertaining. "I love you because you're kind."

And yet how determined we are to destroy what we love.

"I'm not so kind."

"What are you talking about? Look at what you do with your life. The people you help."

A diversionary tactic. A shapeless white jacket, an embroidered name, a badge. Survival relies on predatory instinct. It's equal parts knowing when to hide and when to reveal yourself. You did this better than anyone, Dan. A hoodie and some paint cans. Someone might have mistaken you for a teenage tagger. But the smile. Your smile. It takes a refined sensibility to identify emotional camouflage. I was too good-hearted. Remember how sweet I was?

"Nah," I said. I ran my fingers through Evan's thinning hair. "I haven't been kind for a very long time."

My iPhone was on the night table, I checked my messages: an invitation to a mental health conference in New Zealand, a reminder from the dentist's hygienist that it was time for a cleaning, Diane confirming lunch. Then I put the phone down, rolled onto my back, and stared at the ceiling. I focused on my own breath. In through the nose. Out through the mouth. In through the nose—*If stars can push through a stucco sky*—out through the mouth.

Then maybe.

But actuality looms. It's tricky like that. It creeps, then crawls. Elapsing into step, one then two. Until the intercom buzzes on a chance afternoon. You get up off the couch, walk over to the intercom, check the image on the screen. A familiar face on an unknown young man. "I'm looking for Evan Douglas."

It waxes, then wanes. Converting into memory, close and distant. Resurfacing in present time. On the newsstand outside the market. An image on the cover of the paper. A gaunt man, still. Even more now, perhaps. His haunted eyes. God damn. Really? Jim Carroll died? With all that he'd been through, he had twenty-eight more years than you.

I can feel the pages of the book against my thumb. A paperback. The edges worn. Dog-eared.

"Little kids shoot marbles
where the branches break the sun

into graceful shafts of light . . .
I just want to be pure."

Is that what this was all about? That you wanted to be pure? That's not enough, Dan. That's not enough to justify you leaving me.

Actuality resurrects, then morphs. Alternating appearance. Hoodie and cords, now flannel and denim. Two weeks out. With a new haircut. Neat. Short. You tell yourself that he seems expectant. Shaven. Somewhere between eager and willing. Bright eyed. And he is. Jim. Working on finishing a piece he owes *The Atlantic*. An essay about the biological necessity of fearing death.

"The basic premise," he says, "is that fear is a survival skill. People who forget to fear death become too hopeful."

"What's wrong with that?" I ask.

"Hope makes a person sloppy."

"That's not the end of the world."

"Sure it is. Sloppy people forget about things. They forget to wash their hands after cleaning a chicken. They leave their sneakers in the middle of the floor. Sloppy people," he points to the street outside my window, "neglect to look both ways and get hit by cars."

We are almost out of time. Excellent news for someone prone to escape.

"I'm happy to run over. I don't have anyone until eleven."

"Thanks so much," he says. His smile charming. "But I can't." Jim pulls his sweater down over his head, signaling that the conversation is over. "Tuesday? Same time, same station?"

I nod my head up and down.

"Eight-thirty, Tuesday morning." He plugs the date and time into his phone. "In fact, I'll bring the coffee next time. How do you like it?"

I imagine there is a significant amount of fear in my eyes. "A hint of milk. Three teaspoons of sugar."

But he doesn't allow his eyes to rest on mine. "So, a hint of milk. Three teaspoons of sugar." He punches those details into his phone as well. "You got it. Eight-thirty, Tuesday."

I tuck my pencil behind my ear and walk over to the door. "It's great to see you're doing so well."

He accuses me of lying then. No, not lying exactly. He questions my certainty, not my intention.

"You must be a terrible card player."

"Really, why's that?"

"Because whenever you're nervous, you do that—it's your tell."

"What is?"

"You tuck a pencil, sometimes a pen, whatever you're using to write with—you tuck it behind your ear."

"But I always—" which, I realize now, was his point.

Jim smiles. "I know you do." He takes the pencil from behind my ear and hands it to me.

Actuality succumbs. It's tricky like that. It lingers, then bows out of your office and into the cool autumn air.

A solitary figure. A man and his dog.

Dogs.

One big, one small, both rescued, walking beside him. Jim stops at the corner. Looks right, then left, then right again. Safe to cross.

Which he does. A difficult activity, he thinks, for a man whose brain is on fire. He hates the way this sounds. The self-pity. The presumption. Still, he continues forward. One foot, followed by the other.

Jim parks the dogs just outside the door, promises to be right back. "Be right back, guys." A simple sentence for a complex gesture. Returning.

Inside, looking out, he can see them. One licks himself. The other itches. There is an innocence to their faith and there is real beauty in that. Eyes without fear. A cappuccino and the *Times*. He pays, have a nice day, green into the tip jar. His gestures obligatory more than thoughtful.

The dogs wag their tails when they see him. This makes him smile. He and Cindy have given two mutts a home. That's more than most people. Certainly more than most dogs have the right to ask for. "Let's go play," he says, patting the top of their heads. He is sensitive to the touch, the palm of his right hand.

At the dog run he unleashes them, takes the familiar green ball from his hip pocket and throws it. The little dog gets to the ball first, which makes him laugh. Jim loves these dogs. This he is sure of. If he ever loved anything, it's these dogs.

Later. Back home now. Cindy calls to check up on him. "How was your day?"

"Good," he answers. He finished the piece. And yes, that is great, but it isn't something to celebrate. Not yet anyway. "Let's see if they like it." The "they" he is referring to is ostensibly the people at *The Atlantic* but Cindy knows the "they" is the absolution from a language he cannot master. A red kickball puncturing a blue sky. The forgiving touch of a razor's edge.

"I'm on my way home, need anything?"

"Some chips and a Dr Pepper would be great."

She says, "No problem. Back in twenty. Can't wait to see who wins. I think it's going to be the little girl in the rhinestone cowboy boots."

He says something like "Me too," even though he knows she's lost to the fire-eater. Flame trumping sparkle. DVR, time. As he hangs up the phone, he disconnects the cable wire, making this doubly cruel.

Jim passes several photographs on the way to the kitchen. He glances at them but he doesn't have to. He knows the images: A wedding shot. A camping trip. A Polaroid of a little boy in overalls. Him in overalls, age six, maybe seven. First grade.

There is a small patio behind their apartment. A table and two chairs. The table and chairs are why they fell in love with the place. He and Cindy would enjoy breakfasts at that table, share the Sunday paper, a pot of coffee. And talk. Past. Present. Future. Which they did. His chair facing the sun. Hers the shade.

He makes his way out back. Shapes the noose. Secures the wire. Places the chair. Each movement has purpose. Last fall he and Cindy carved a pumpkin right over there. Last winter they built a little snowman. Jim doesn't hear the echo of their laughter, only the quiet din of certainty. He steps onto the seat of the chair, one foot followed by the other. He takes a deep breath; habit not doubt. Then he kicks the chair. The same two dogs, one big, one small, both rescued, bearing witness.

I knew. NOT WHAT PRECISELY. I CAN'T SAY I KNEW JIM WAS dead but I knew he wasn't showing up with coffee. Still, I went through the motions. I put my bag on the chair, sorted the mail, turned on the AC. No, it was a nice day. I cracked the window, switched on the lamp, checked in with my service. But by eight thirty-five I knew. It's not like I'm psychic or anything. We all know, somewhere inside every goodbye is the knowledge that it might not be goodbye-for-now but goodbye forever. An oil slick, an aneurysm, a convenience store robbery. But this was different. This was the brand of knowing that buffers the mind by shutting it down. I began sharpening pencils. I was on the third pencil when the phone rang, the fourth when I answered it.

"Hello?"

No words were exchanged. Obstructed by grief, Cindy's breath hung dormant, then a slight wheeze.

"When?" I heard myself ask. In an attempt to belie panic and because I'd been through it enough times to know that it didn't really matter "when," my voice was measured. It's funny, you'd think it would matter, Dan, the "when," but it doesn't. The "how" doesn't matter much either. Some are easier to accept than others. Overdose, leap-off-bridge, blade-slicing-wrist. You can, if you are someone who can bend logic to fit need, convince yourself it was an accident, a cry-for-help gone wrong.

Noose, not so much. Noose takes preparation. Shotgun, serious business. Your technique, I'll hand it to you, was somewhat unique, which made it a bit more challenging to decode. There's an ostensible impulsivity in fire. Biblical even. Would you prefer I call you Belteshazzar?

For Cindy, if religion failed to serve its purpose, history might redeem her. Pattern establishes inevitability. Classification offers context. Narrative builds emotional scaffolding. And so we exist. Compartmentalizing pain. Memory by memory. Brick by brick.

When Cindy opened the front door, everything looked the same as it always did. Jim's shoes lying where they'd been kicked off, one this way, one that. His wallet in the bowl on the front console. Dog leashes on the hook. She chuckled when she saw the McDonald's bag. The fries were gone but Jim had left half the burger for her. A peace offering of sorts. She picked up the burger, shouted playfully, "You're in so much trouble, you big baby. You didn't leave me any fries." Then took a bite.

Later she said part of her must have known. Because she didn't like burgers and she especially didn't like Big Macs. Thoughts passed through her mind. It was odd that Jim hadn't come to the kitchen. Why was Sandy scratching at the door? Cindy took another bite and then another until there was nothing left to chew. Only then did she put her bags down, shout, "I'm coming, Sandy." She opened the door and scooped the dog into her arms. "Where's your brother?" She kissed Sandy's belly. "Where's Igor? And where's Daddy?"

Daddy.

Only now, with Sandy in her arms, did her mind consent and allow her to glance at her husband across the patio. Hanging. Flannel and denim. His feet just two, maybe three inches off the ground.

Jim's body was pitched in such a way that he could have, in an alternate reality, been mid-step. "Hey, babe," a quick kiss, and then from behind his back, "Abracadabra," a red fry box with a golden *M*. "Did you really think I'd eat all the fries?"

Again Cindy's mind protected her, protects her. She has no recollection of what happened after. How she got Jim down. When she called 911. Cindy sees Igor by her feet and then sees Jim's head resting on her lap. She feels her fingers run through his hair. She hears herself say, "Open your eyes." Then plead. "Please. Please open your eyes."

And this, Dan, is why I say the "when" and "how" don't really matter. Because Jim wouldn't open his eyes. Not then. Not ever.

I said, "I'm so sorry, Cindy."

I said, "No, there was nothing more you could have done."

I said, "Thank you for calling."

And then I felt myself running. I felt myself running and knew I shouldn't be running. I had no place to run to. No person to reach. Yet, I slowed only to start again. This went on for quite some time until I finally stopped. A seat on a bench. A neighborhood playground. A sandbox.

And that's when I saw them, just outside the gate. There they were, lining up for peaches—vacant, innocent eyes— we're not supposed to say "retarded" anymore, so I won't. But them. The "intellectually disabled" cretins. Single file. Waiting on line for an autumn peach. One had escaped and was running toward the playground. His primitive voice demonic. A mother leapt off the bench, another shouted, "Anna, come out of the sandbox." No need to worry. A guardian of some sort, wearing an intense yellow Hope House T-shirt, led the boy away by the arm. "You are too big to play in a sandbox, Dwayne," he said.

This to someone's son. Some mother who, for these few hours a day, walks through the world unadorned by grief. She could be any woman running down the steps, hopping on the subway, late for a meeting. Without Dwayne by her side, people cut her in line, push her aside, even look her in the eyes. A momentary escape from shame, which leaves her feeling fraudulent. That she should take a step on earth untethered to the stone. A heinous act, bringing a person into the world only to abandon him.

Dwayne's mother lives each day aware that when she dies—which she will, sooner rather than later—there will be no one to look after him. And people on the street see this too. That she has a boy who will grow up only to live full-time in a home, an assisted-living facility, where once every summer he, now a man-boy, with a receding hairline and suspenders, will stand in line and wait for a peach. A late summer peach. This his nineteenth summer harvest.

Feel it, the fur against his lips, the juice on his tongue, the flesh in his teeth.

If you don't I'll tell it to you again.

And still it happened anyway.

I took A BREATH BEFORE VIEWING THE OPEN CASKET. NECK burns are easy to camouflage as long as the deceased's eyes are closed. And so he appeared at peace in the box, Jim did. Peaceful yet solid. Barrel-chested, a full head of hair. Jim, putting aside for a moment that he was dead, looked durable. The age men in their sixties envy. Still enough strength and time to actualize: lower golf handicap, new baby, convertible. And yet he didn't, or couldn't—Jim simply couldn't visualize the distance between himself and the destination. Or perhaps he could but instead chose not to invest in the "mirage."

His word.

Which perhaps it is, joy.

I spotted Cindy across the room. Those must be Jim's parents sitting next to her. He was a real combination. The same broad shoulders as his father, the fine features of his mother. They would be flying him home soon. Just after the service. A small cemetery about twenty minutes from their home. Cindy was okay with it. Jim didn't believe in God and she didn't believe in God so much either so it didn't really matter where his body went. But Jim's parents did. They believed in God, hell and resurrection. So for them it would mean something to have him close. They could have lunch together. The Archers and their boy.

"Remember," Mrs. Archer could say to her husband over ham and cheese sandwiches, "how he used to wear his Batman cape to the carwash?" She might smile then. Look at Jimmy waving his arms in the air, pretending he can fly. To think nothing happened to him. Leaning out the station wagon window, with no seatbelt on. A yard of black polyester, half a yard of yellow felt. How easy it was to make him happy then.

Her thoughts travel to her spiffy new Berina. Jim and Cindy gave it to her on her sixty-fifth birthday. It was Cindy's idea. "For all the Halloween costumes you're going to make," she said as Jim placed the large box on the kitchen table. And she would have done that, Mrs. Archer. Nothing would have given her more pleasure. Forget Halloween. What about a set of bumpers for the crib, a baby quilt for a stroller—a little linen dress with rosettes? Oh my gosh, how cute would that be.

Cindy stood as I approached, "Thank you so much for coming. Jim would have been . . ."

What? I thought to myself. What would Jim have been, Cindy? Happy that I was here? I failed him. I failed her. I failed all of them for that matter, everyone who loved him. Just as I failed you. And it made no sense to me. Nothing about my life made any sense to me anymore. If I couldn't save Jim what was the point?

I glanced at Jim's mom. Her eyes had begun darting about the room. Look at all these people gaping at her boy's dead body. This is unacceptable, for him to be exposed like this. And she wasn't doing anything to protect him. She was just sitting there. And it was going to be time soon.

Five minutes.

There weren't going to be bumpers or linen dresses.

Ten minutes at the most.

They will sprinkle some holy water, close the coffin and she won't ever see him again . . . but he'll be close by. Less than twenty minutes away. She can visit him every day if she wants. There are flowers to plant in the spring. Leaves to be swept away in the fall.

And that's when I heard it, Dan. The familiar yet nearly inaudible sound of defeat.

The first time I met Jim he said, "I listened to the voice that said not to, until I couldn't hear it anymore. No, that's not it—it's not that I couldn't hear it. It was just quieter than the other voice. The voice that said 'You must.' 'Must' being a directive without caveats. That voice, the louder one, made a noise—a hissing sound—that burrowed into the underside of my skull. A captive giant thrusting his massive palms into the edges of my mind, which made me worry, knowing instinctively that there is only so far a mind can stretch before it shatters. Shards of regret ricocheting about the room. One settled, neither impartial nor personal, in the vein of my right forearm. 'You again,' I said before submerging myself head-first into a tub filled with water the consistency of Milk of Magnesia. I pressed my nose into the nonslip pad. 'I will silence you,' I vowed. 'You will be silenced.'"

Jim took a breath, ran his thumb over his wrist. His scar a doorway into the abyss. "I awoke in the shade of a trompe l'oeil lemon tree. If God gives you lemons, make lemonade, right? The thing is, lemonade is sweet so it doesn't last long." Jim shrugged his shoulders.

"'Fool' the Giant answered, close-fisted, eager to ignite rage. It was right around then that I began to wear this navy bandana. I belted it around my temples, pulling it tight. I would jail the Giant. The Giant would no longer be an active guest. And the Giant wasn't for quite some time."

I took a seat toward the back of the chapel and waited for the room to fill. I'm still early to everything. You were always late. There were theories, remember? If you organized your time better. Went to bed at a more decent hour. Took traffic into account. All valid suggestions proffered by well-meaning people suitably versed in napkin-on-the-lap protocol. But the thing is, what I understood, even back then, Dan, was that your being late had nothing to do with time. You divided your world into two groups. Those who waited for you and those who left. If a person cared enough, if seeing you was important enough to them, they'd wait.

I always waited.

And remain outside, looking in. Memory witnessed through transparent glass. You are just beyond my reach. A figure in a snow globe. You loom, then vanish, only to reemerge. Infinitesimally small. So small that you are no longer the figure in the little house on the hill but the snow itself. Drifting downward. One flake. Slow. Steady.

There is something comforting about living in a contained atmosphere, under a dome, an object in another person's creation. Standing next to an evergreen, on a sailboat, under the Hollywood sign. I would choose to be the tiny figure in the castle tower, perhaps. A purple castle with a moat. Or a tourist at a tourist destination. Paris. The wide-eyed figure waiting at the base of the Eiffel Tower. In springtime, no less. Yet it will snow. It always snows in a snow globe.

I'm outside looking in and I see you carrying an old wooden toy box over to your bed. Inside the box are bombing supplies: spray paint, markers, caps. You check your inventory against the blueprint in your sketchbook. Tonight you are using greens: Mint Green, Avocado, Teal. You don't have the Avocado, so you replace it with School Bus Yellow. You wrap the cans in a couple of T-shirts so they don't clang, place them in a small duffel bag, toss in some markers, a baggie of caps, and return the box to its hiding spot in your closet. I ask you where you're going. You say, "New Lots." I ask if I can go with you. You say, "It's not a good idea," but you don't say, "No."

I'm outside looking in and I see Ray waiting for us at the foot of a sleeping car. I follow you down the tracks. What we're doing is against the law, but we don't care because we're young and bursting with certitude. About what I'm still not sure. Maybe it was simply the sheer audacity of the undertaking. You and Ray compare plans. Ray's utilizes color. Yours scale. Tonight you will exploit both. AJAX and JAKYL. Bright and loud. Declaration and warning.

I'm outside looking in and I see us. It's still early in the summer. Warm but not too warm. We are sitting on a bench, waiting for the sun to rise, our train to pass. So we can see last night's creation. Acrylic paint on a tin canvas. We are sharing an apple pie from McDonald's. Ray opens the box, "I wonder who came up with the idea to shape it like a rectangle." He offers me the pie but I refuse. He smiles, takes a bite, passes it to you. You take a bite, "And more importantly who thought to deep-fry it."

"It was the Force for sure." There's real edge in my voice.

"Suze," you say, "why are you still all bent out of shape about this?"

"I just disagree with you guys."

"Suze, Luke chokes two Gamorrean guards at the start of the movie."

"That doesn't mean he turned to the Dark Side, Dan."

"Ray, please explain it to her." You take a tiny pipe out of your pocket and pack a bowl. "My sister is being willingly ignorant."

"All he's saying, Suze, is that anger is toxic to a Jedi. The movie starts and Luke's sorta consumed with anger. It's not like he just chokes those guards. He threatens Jabba. Lashes out at the Emperor. Instigates the last duel with Vader."

You repack the pipe, take a hit, and say, "He also begs Darth Vader to save his life while the Emperor is electrocuting him."

"I don't get why that's bad."

"Because Jedi never beg for their lives. Look at Obi-Wan Kenobi! He accepts his death and gracefully surrenders to the Force."

"There's nothing graceful in surrendering, Daniel. Obi's dead."

We hear the train and stand. Even from this distance we can see it. Green letters on a roaming tin canvas.

"Damn, that looks cool," you say.

"Yeah," I say, "it's pretty amazing."

Ray smiles. "Are you two ready to make up?"

You put your arm around me, both as a sign of affection and because you are so stoned you can barely walk. "You're right, Suze. Vader would never have let Luke give in even if some part of him wanted him to." And I understand then that we were never really talking about Darth Vader.

I am outside looking in. It's the middle of the summer now. We are hanging out on the roof. It's one of those perfect nights. The sky's clear and from up high the entire city stretches out before us. To the west a lone tugboat guides a massive cargo ship to safety. Out east, tall, well-lit buildings stand erect, as if protesting gravity. Uptown the bridge sparkles, tempting escape. And to the south, Lady Liberty, torch in hand, keeps guard, bearing witness.

Tiny has his boom box. Margo brought some pot. All

around us lamps dim in unison with the sleepy breath of their owners. Ray comes barreling up the fire escape, a newspaper in his hands. He reads to us: "'Yesterday, Ed Koch, the mayor of New York City, reaffirmed his 'war on graffiti.' According to Koch, train yards will be surrounded by barbed wire, sewer covers will have locks; security is being beefed up across the board. 'By the time I'm done, the only animals running below ground be will be rats, and we'll get them too,' Koch said." Ray deepened his voice: "'This warning hasn't deterred a new generation of taggers.

"'If you ride the subway system, you are familiar with the names AJAX and JAKYL. Like Taki 183 and Dondi before them, AJAX and JAKYL are on a quest to become All-City.

"'Their names have been seen on nearly every train line in every borough of New York City. Why do they do it? What is it they are trying to say and why are they risking their freedom to say it?'" Ray turns to Daniel, "What are you trying to say, JAKYL?"

I am outside looking in. It's the end of summer now. We are on our backs, arms and legs touching. We gaze at the moon. Margo thinks the moon is hanging especially low. "It wants to shake your hand. It wants to congratulate you, Daniel."

"For what?"

"For becoming All-City."

You give Margo a quick, gentle kiss on the lips. "One more."

Margo whispers something into your ear. You smile. Even in the moonlight your cheeks glow pink. I can see everything so clearly. Tiny with his boom box. Margo in that red off-the-shoulder blouse. We lie on our backs, arms and legs touching, and stare into the black city sky. Ray passes me a joint, which I take a hit off of, and hand to you, who take a good, long toke before passing it to Margo. Tiny plays "Tangerine" and Plant's voice wafts through the night sky. Somehow I know it's the end before it really is the end. I think somehow we all did.

Meanwhile, on the other side of town, a twenty-five-year-old black man named Michael Stewart was leaving work and heading home to Clinton Hill. Later in newspaper articles and on TV they would refer to him as a graffiti artist, which is ridiculous. Michael Stewart wasn't like you, Dan. He never sat on the bench at 149th, wielded an aerosol can, had a book. He was a 135-pound guy with a sharpie marker who doodled.

Amateurs like Michael Stewart made it bad for guys like you and Ray. Bombers who spent days sketching, thinking color, perfecting design. You wanted to create something that blew people's minds. You wanted every coffee-sipping, doughnut-eating commuter to smile on his or her way to work. To say "Look what those crazy motherfuckers did this time." But Koch had declared war on graffiti, and like any war, the enemy rarely stops to question. And so we hung out on our roof, smoking pot, listening to Led Zeppelin, as eleven police officers beat Michael Stewart into a coma.

But Michael Stewart didn't die instantly. For ten days he lay in a coma in Bellevue Hospital. It was during that time that you prepared yourself for death. People, I learned then, busy themselves with all sorts of things.

I wasn't outside looking in any longer. I was at Jim's funeral. My patient Jim Archer. Forty-six years old. Jim Archer who began taking medication for depression in college. Who stayed on that medication for over twenty years despite the sweating, migraines, debilitating nausea. So it wasn't entirely irrational when, newly married and stable, Jim decided to try one of the new-generation antidepressants. They had so many less side effects. And things were different now. He had a steady teaching job, an estimable career, a wife who loved him. Wouldn't this constancy insulate him against a potential onslaught?

The chatter started again as chatter does. One day, under the covers, goosenecked and lonely, Jim listened as foreign correspondents promised peace was in the region. He knew that this was different. This was something other. Day and night merged into printed documents. Character. Theme. Meaning. Beginning. Middle. End.

He was in a race to finish. Linked novellas: *Simple Noise*, *Jacob's View of the Solar System from a Twin Size Bed*, *The Butterfly Effect*. Sixty-four thousand, three hundred and ninety-two words.

Jim printed out the manuscript and placed it on top of his desk. Then he counted out the pills he'd been able to save.

Twenty-four pills, Jim thought. Sixty-four thousand, three hundred and ninety-two words. *Twenty-four pills should do it.* And they probably would have if Cindy hadn't happened to come home early that day.

"Can you help him, Dr. Seliger?"

This time around nothing worked. The new SSRI. The old MAOI. The currents of electricity that I ran through his brain. Sure, Jim had a tiny reprieve, a few days where he "remembered what it was like to be happy." A slice of pizza. A hot bath. A solid card game. But those brief moments did little to offset his despair. Jim was certain that if he continued with the treatment, his mind would crack. But it didn't crack, Dan, it merely surrendered.

"**Excuse me.**" Two men were trying to get to their seats. I stood and made room. After the men squeezed past, they began to exchange pleasantries—"When do you think it will start?", "Look how many people are here"—common practice at such an occasion. The older of the two men, a columnist at *The New York Times*. The other, an editor for *The New Yorker*. Both had worked closely with Jim. Both were deeply saddened. And how did I know Jim?

"He's an old friend."

"From Louisiana?" the editor asked.

"Yes," I said, "family friend." Lying, generally considered a character defect, can actually be essential to survival.

Cindy made her way to the podium. She looked smaller than I remembered. Too small to have taken on the enormous task of keeping Jim alive.

"Thanks so much for coming," she said, then cleared her throat. "On our first date, Jim took me to the hot-dog-eating contest in Coney Island. I don't know how in the world I left that impression on him—that I was the kind of girl who liked hot-dog-eating contests—since we met picking up vegetarian Thai. But that was Jim.

"For those of you who don't know, every year Nathan's hosts a hot-dog-eating contest on the Fourth of July. And it's a big deal. People come from all over to see who's able to shove the most hot dogs down their throat. On the train ride over, Jim brought me up to date. He explained that it happened to be a particularly exciting year because the year before, six-time defending champion Takeru Kobayashi was upset by relative newcomer Joey "Jaws" Chestnut. Jim said, 'So, Cindy, the question is this: Will Chestnut get to keep the Mustard Belt for another year or have to relinquish it to Kobayashi?' He wasn't joking. The competition was fierce. And it turned out to be a real nail-biter. Kobayashi and Chestnut went hot dog for hot dog. It ended in a tie. Both downed fifty-nine hot dogs in ten minutes. Which is nearly six hot dogs a minute." Cindy chuckled to herself. "But Joey Chestnut prevailed, defending his title in a five-hot-dog eat-off in overtime. Jim prevailed as well, because he got me to take a bite of his hot dog—'One bite for me, one bite for you, and we'll throw the rest out'—which was my first bite of meat, if you can call it that, in twenty years. After the hot-dog-eating contest, we played some arcade games—Jim won me a small stuffed turtle—and we rode the roller coaster. That night in front of my apartment he kissed me for the first time. And I've been a meat eater ever since."

Cindy glanced at the audience, smiled slightly, and continued. "A couple days later, Jim and I decided to cook our first meal together." Cindy waited a beat. "Barbequed ribs. We went to the market to buy the ribs, and the woman at the register had these amazing painted fingernails. They were bright turquoise and one of them had a pink flamingo on it. As someone who's been a chronic nail biter her whole life, I said, 'Wow, your nails are amazing.' She looked up at me and smiled. 'Thanks,' she said. I helped her pack the bags. Wished her a nice day.

"There was nothing particularly unusual about this exchange. But as soon as we walked out of the market, Jim said, 'You gotta be careful with that.'

"I had no idea what he was talking about. 'Who you look at in the eyes. It could be deadly.'

"'Deadly?'

"'Sure. To know what's going on in someone else's mind. Say that woman at the register had just found out her sister had heart disease and without a heart transplant she was going to die. There you were having a perfectly fine day. Your eyes meet and suddenly, as if a brick fell from the beak of a flying bird, you are struck to the ground. Annihilated. Because the woman's eyes, this stranger's eyes, lead you to the recess, to the darkest cavity of the mind, where death can no longer masquerade as turquoise painted fingernails. There, even the strongest powers of denial are rendered obsolete. And you are reminded that you are going to die. That we are all going to die.'

"At first I thought Jim was joking, but I quickly realized that he was being serious. And that's how he told me. Or rather how I experienced it for the first time. His desolation. It would come and go and in some ways became a third person in our relationship. We referred to it as Black Bear. Jim would say, 'Seems like Black Bear is rummaging through the trash tonight,' and I'd understand that he was having a hard time.

"For some reason, and God knows I've spent hours upon hours trying to figure out what it was—that we moved in together, that he was eating mostly home-cooked meals, that the writing was going well—Jim was given a pardon. For over a year he was stable. We would talk about the depression, how it felt when he was a kid, what it felt like as a teenager, later, now. We began, not making light of it, but not fearing it as much. I guess you could say we were sanguine. 'Black Bear's still sleeping,' I'd say. And he'd smile, 'Let's pray it's a long winter.'

"We were happy. Really happy. I'm trying to take solace in that. That we were happy."

Cindy reached into her pocket, "Jim left me a note and I want to share part of it with you." She unfolded a sheet of notebook paper, leaned into the podium, cleared her throat. "I have one last thought, Cind. Don't be mad at the dogs. They tried to stop me. They are trying now. Igor is wagging his tail, Sandy is following me around the house with his sad, brown saucer eyes. I amend an earlier statement. Don't look people *or dogs* in the eyes. Perhaps especially dogs. And don't be mad at yourself for stopping at the deli. There are no what-ifs in this scenario. I insisted you bring me home a bag of chips."

Cindy's voice cracked, and she began to whimper. "I'm sorry. Please bear with me."

She took a moment.

"I have really bad insomnia. Have had it as long as I can remember. Jim being Jim, he decided he was going to cure it. So he came up with this game. He called it 'Picture This.' We'd be in bed and he'd say, 'You asleep?' and I'd say, 'No,' and he'd say, 'Picture this?' And he'd bring me into his arms. 'Okay, person, place or thing?' If I said 'Place,' he'd pick the Indian Ocean, say, or Paris. A ski slope. Each time the place was different but the characters were the same. A man and woman who were madly in love.

"Once I said, 'Thing,' and Jim told me a story about a turtle named Leon who discovered he had wings while he was the ring boy—ring turtle, rather—for this same man and woman, who by the way were not only madly in love but looked remarkably like me and Jim." Cindy smiled. "Anyway, it was taking Leon forever to get down the aisle, and he was so eager to deliver them their rings he suddenly began to fly. Sometimes the Picture This worked and Jim's cockamamie story would put me to sleep, but mostly he'd fall asleep as he was telling it to me. And I remember thinking, not once, but every night that we had together, that we were so lucky to have found each other. And I'm trying to take solace in this too. That we were madly in love.

"Anyway, tonight when I close my eyes, I'm going to play Picture This. I'm going to picture Jim on a mountaintop. Leon's there with him and they are cooking hot dogs over a fire pit. Leon rolls over on his shell back and Jim tickles his belly and smiles. As most of you know, Jim was an atheist, so this isn't my vision of him in heaven. It's just what I imagine peace would look like for Jim. You know, if I knew Jim found peace it would almost be worth the price of having to live the rest of my life without him."

I so much wanted this to be true for Cindy. That she could find a way to justify Jim's death and move on. No, not just move on, but live a full life, thrive even. I had known Cindy for less than a year, and throughout the whole time, she had remained bright-eyed, thoughtful, and sweet. What a crime it would be if Jim stole that from her. I remember looking at her standing up there, trying her best to put the audience at ease, and thinking she had a chance to be okay. Her generosity of spirit might just save her.

I didn't possess Cindy's grace. It never occurred to me to consider whether you were happier dead or alive. All I could think about, all I wanted to know, was why. Why in the world you left me here.

I spent the morning of your funeral lying on your bed staring at the ray of light that spread across your ceiling. I was certain you were trying to send me a message. I spent decades like this. Misinterpreting shadows. What I realized over time is that the morning of your funeral was like any other autumn morning. All that was on your ceiling was a line of light. A line that led nowhere but into itself again.

Mom came into the room and asked what she could bring me. "What can I get you, Suze?" Somehow she had been able to get herself dressed and ready to bury you, and I hated her for it. I had read in some magazine that if you really want to punish someone, ignore them; so I didn't answer. But I knew what I wanted, Dan.

I wanted to sit on your bed, knees to chest, and listen to you vent about what a dick Coach Ross was and how your civil rights teacher, Mr. Robbins, was actually a racist and why Pat Benatar was hotter than Joan Jett. I wanted you to let me tag along after school. I wanted to smoke one of your clove cigarettes, listen to "Freebird," and help you choose a birthday present for Margo. I wanted us to go to the movies. Share a big bag of popcorn with melted Sno-Caps. I wanted to sneak into your room in the middle of the night, lie down on the floor, and wait for you to toss me a blanket and pillow. I wanted you to tell me that I shouldn't be scared. That it was all a bad dream. That if I closed my eyes and went to sleep, everything would be back to normal the following morning.

Can you get me that, Ma?

Jim's mother and father made their way to the podium. Jim's father said, "Eve and I have a million stories about Jim, and while they won't be enough—nothing will ever be enough to fill this gaping void—we will use them, as best we can, to sustain us. Eve and I wanted to share this one with you."

George planted his elbows and leaned into the microphone. "A little boy"—his voice quavered—"when Jimmy was a little boy, not much taller than a fire hydrant, he would stand with his back to the park fence. He was three, four years old, which seems young in the abstract, too young for baseball, but there he was: knees bent, ready position. 'Trow me!' He still had problems with the 'th' sound. 'Trow me, Daddy.' I would smile, wind my arm, a dramatic gesture that would make Jimmy laugh, and throw him the ball. But one day—I don't know, maybe a year or two later—he stood at attention, his dark eyes focused on the palm of my hand. Jimmy waited for the release and scrambled to catch the ball. He grabbed it with his free hand but before chucking it back he said, 'Trow one I can't catch, Daddy!' There was accusation in his voice; he thought I was being easy on him and he didn't like this. So I threw him a pop fly the next time. It was slightly higher than the last ball, but that little guy managed to catch it just the same. 'Daddy!'

"This went on for years. Day in, day out. I would throw and Jimmy would ask me to 'trow harder' and then 'throw harder.' What he never understood, as a boy, or as a man, was that there was no ball I could throw that he wouldn't be able to catch. I told him this, but Jimmy, not willing to accept the limitations of my arm, never believed it."

Outside, the WEATHER WAS UNUSUALLY COLD FOR THE SEA-son. I headed west, then north along the Hudson. Sailboats, cargo ships, tugboats drifting with purpose. Each reliant on an external energy to propel forward. I got to the boat basin around four. A woman in a mauve robe stood on the deck of her houseboat. "Good afternoon to you," she said, gesturing her mug in my direction. It was one of those plastic mugs, the kind mom used to drink out of. No, not plastic, melamine. White melamine. A large white melamine mug with a thin lip and a wide groove in the handle. I see her then, Mom, spoon-ing two teaspoons of instant coffee into the mug. Taster's Choice. I'm pretty sure that's what it was, Taster's Choice in-stant coffee, the jar had a red cap remember?

And then there she is taking the kettle off the stove and pouring the scalding water into the mug—steam rising—which is the only way she would drink her coffee. It wasn't hot enough if she couldn't feel the steam warming her cheeks as she took a sip. She would sit at the kitchen table with the paper, running her thumb along the handle of the mug with her right hand, turning the pages with her left. There are so many things we don't even know we've forgotten.

I smiled back at the lady on the houseboat and continued along my way, walking, exchanging pleasantries with strangers, a nod of the head, a curl of the upper lip, as if it were an ordinary day because it was an ordinary day. The magnificent and tragic happen on ordinary days. Three hundred and sixty-five to be exact. And so time passes, years in fact, with all sorts of things happening around us to all sorts of people. The agglomeration of which we call life. My life. His life. Her life.

Yours.

Your life, Dan.

Every so often I get to escape the present day. We all do, the living. The chance melamine flash and we relive what was lost to us. Which is what I needed more than anything on the ordinary day that was Jim's funeral. The chance to see you again.

And so I reached our spot, which was, to my surprise, no longer a small cluster of boulders but a patch of freshly laid sod. I placed my jacket on the ground and sat down. Across the river, newly constructed townhouses were flanked by optimistic trees. Yes, even in Jersey. What gall. To climb toward sunlight on a cloud-filled afternoon.

It's almost funny, right Dan? Soft-tissue faith. Osseous regret. The mortal and our fractured lives. We return again and again, all of us who have landed here. Purgatory, the space between sun and earth. We still below a cloudy pink sky as the encircling sewage conjures. Spray-paint and Lifesavers. Weed. We beg the omniscient air to liberate dialogue.

"Do you ever get scared of falling?"

We pretend to believe that if we close our eyes hard enough, if we imagine deep enough, then we might find something to clutch onto. A fluttering of the eye, an intonation in the voice, an answer.

"No. I'm never scared of falling."

And then there you are.

We touch.

Fingertip to fingertip.

I say, "Where have you been?"

You say, "Here the whole time."

I am happy to make the conceit. I hand you a Dr Pepper, lean back onto my elbows, and listen as you expound on the various injustices in the world. I nod my head in agreement as you explain why Hart and not Mould is the heart (excuse the pun) of Hüsker Dü and how it was actually smart of Duran to have quit the fight with Leonard because that was actually the braver thing to do and how your next piece, the piece that's going to make you officially All-City, is going to be a mural in honor of the black kid that got beaten up on the subway a few nights before.

I don't mention that Ray thinks that the tension between Hart and Mould stems from them having had some kind of lovers' quarrel and that Hart, being a heroin addict, doesn't help the situation. I don't remind you that you used to say Duran was bloated and out of shape and that's why he quit. I don't try to stop you from doing the piece. I don't say that it's too dangerous, that it won't change a thing, that there will always be police brutality. I don't mention that a year after you fell to your death, a little old black lady named Eleanor Bumpers will be killed by some cop for essentially not paying her rent. Because this is my alternative version of truth. Where you are celebrated on microfilm. And we grow old together.

You know what happens when someone dies, Daniel? People continue to eat, shit, and fuck. A new cargo ship comes along. Life resumes. More goods that will never be consumed: Band-Aids, bottles of beer, nail polish. I look at my hands. My nails, the same Bordeaux as Mom's. When they stopped making this color, Mom searched every pharmacy in the city. I found a case of them for her on eBay. There were eleven unopened boxes when she died.

Just because I can picture you all alone in this world doesn't mean it won't happen.

She was slicing a piece of pound cake down the center. Lemon, with the white icing that you and I love. I had just returned from eight years in Seattle where I worked under Dr. Moore, a pioneer in electroconvulsive therapy. I went there, ostensibly, to save lives. But in truth I went there for only one reason, to save my own.

Now I was back in New York City and Mom wanted me to call Ray. To meet him and apologize. But it wasn't fair I said. To do that to Ray. Walk in and out of his life at leisure.

She offered me half of the piece of pound cake but I didn't want any so she pushed it away. She was the type of person that could do that, push the other half away. "Why isn't it fair?" she asked.

"Because he's probably moved on by now."

"Probably or hopefully?" she asked.

"Both." I answered.

And that's when she said it again, "You know Susanna, just because I can picture you all alone in this world doesn't mean it won't happen."

"No, Ma. It doesn't."

A young woman, early thirties, parked her stroller, unbuckled her baby, and sat down next to me. "It's a nice day," she said. The baby, in a yellow t-shirt and denim overalls, smiled at me. "He likes you."

"He's adorable," I said. "How old is he?"

"Six months."

"My gosh, he's so big for his age."

"His dad is six four."

"That explains it."

The baby cooed at me. I cooed back.

I was scared she was going to ask me how many kids I have, so I checked my watch and said, "Wow. I can't believe the time." Grabbed my jacket and bag. "I've got to get home. Nice to meet you." Smiled one last time at the baby and hurried away.

There are chat rooms devoted to women who don't care. Women who, if asked how many kids they have, could easily say, "I don't have any kids, never wanted to." Who find fulfillment elsewhere. A black Lab, a conference room, a tour bus. But what I realized, what I finally allowed myself to accept, was that I wasn't one of those women. I wanted, I needed, a child to love.

And that was okay.

The day was coming to a close. All around me "time-for-dinner-don't-forget-your-jacket" was being met with "five-more-minutes-I'm-not-hungry." Soon the park would empty. Pouty cherubic faces scootering home. Vacant swings at sunset.

Folded strollers and muddy shoes cast aside for video games and cartoons. Pots filled with water and heated to a boil, vegetables cut, tables set.

A mother stops on her way home from work to buy a quart of milk. A tired babysitter gets ready to return to her own family. A husband's train will be delayed and he'll call home and say, "I'm going to be a little late. Need anything, honey?" And she'll say, "Just for you to get home safe." And he will get home. He'll walk through the door with his key, put down his briefcase, and shout, "Daddy's home!" A small child will hurry out, with a clean face, combed hair, in jammies. There was a whole world out there, Dan. A world I was, and was not, a part of.

You once, in a moment of anger, said all my letters were apology letters. This isn't an apology. Or a letter for that matter. You are dead. I am alive. You can't hear me. Nothing new, really. You couldn't—didn't want to—hear me then.

Begging.

I begged.

And still you walked out the door. Branding a road map in the soft tissue of my brain.

Men leave. All men.

Even the good guys.

A cul-de-sac. A highway.

"Tits and a top hat are the only props I need," one said, fondling my breasts. I was in my early twenties. I-95 North. I appreciated the artifice. A white dove cushioned on a bed of popcorn, his signature trick. I acquiesced. Feigning delight. And waited for him to vanish from my bedroom. Pleasure a primitive illusion.

So this isn't an apology. Well, that's not entirely true. In a way it's an apology to the me I was before. The ghost of me. Slight frame. Fair skin. Brown eyes. Remember how people would stop her on the street? *What pretty eyes . . .* Now she wears sunglasses. Never without sunglasses.

Back then she delighted in drawing lines of white chalk on the sidewalk. Hopscotch—how many boxes? One foot. Two feet. One. Two. One. Two. Turn. She was great at it. She could jump from number to number on one leg. Without hesitation. It's hard for me to imagine she doesn't hopscotch anymore, or play with dolls, or smile.

No, that's a bit melodramatic. I smile. Just not like she did. This doesn't seem to be unreasonable. If I could have warned her, everything might be different. But she didn't see it. The fear in your eyes. No, that's not true. She saw the fear, the panic really, she just didn't understand what it revealed. And so everything happened the way it happened and now everything is the way it is.

And I am who I am.

Yes, if I could apologize to anyone, I'd apologize to me. To the me I was before. The ghost of myself. Adoring little sister, big-eyed and stuffy-nosed. Remember how people would stop Mom on the train when we were kids? *I've never seen a brother and sister so nice to each other.* You died and I rode alone. Funny, right? Just when we could have really gone somewhere together.

If I could apologize to her, then you might be able to hear me, because she, that girl, never existed again without you. But like I said, this isn't an apology.

I'm not saying I didn't hurt a lot of people along the way. I did and I feel very bad about that. About hurting people who tried to love me after. But I'm tired of apologizing, Dan. Yes, I survived. I'm alive. But until you accept my testimony as truth. Until I hear you say it. I will never be free.

On the TRAIN HOME, A PIGEON SAUNTERED INTO MY SUBWAY car. "Move aside," the pigeon said. I moved aside. Ernesto, I thought. Ernesto, the vigilante pigeon from the Upper West Side. If this were a children's story, Ernesto would sneak into a little girl's knapsack, and late at night when her parents were sleeping, he'd pull a chair right up next to the little girl's bed and announce himself. She wouldn't be scared of the bird. In fact, she'd welcome the company. Her parents were getting divorced, she needed a friend. And Ernesto is purple. Her favorite color is purple.

Together, the little girl and her pigeon friend would concoct a plan. Ernesto would hide in the cookie jar. The little girl would ask for a cookie. Mom would open the jar. There would be a shriek, followed by a rescue. Dad racing into the kitchen, seizing the bird, banishing him to the street. And then, like in any good fairy tale, safe at last, the hero and heroine of the story would live happily ever after.

Mission accomplished, the little girl, eyes puddled with tears, would kiss Ernesto just to the right of his beak, then watch as he made his way to the corner. Fortunately, Ernesto wasn't big on flying, so she could map out his path in her mind. First he'd cross to the other side of the street, turn right at the light, bob on over to the subway where he'd start again. Another random knapsack. Another little girl to save.

Ernesto, the vigilante from the 3 train. I didn't admire the real-life pigeon. Ernesto was a dirty bird. But I respected him. It takes a lot of guts to spend your days swaggering, pigeon-toed, in and out of subway cars.

I said, "I wouldn't have believed it if I hadn't seen it myself, Evan. There was a pigeon meandering through my subway car, barrel-chested like he owned the place, and no one said a word. I thought someone would scream or call security, notify the conductor, but nothing."

"People have bigger things to worry about, Suza."

"I guess," I said.

Evan began talking about something else. Playoffs? Yes, the playoffs were starting and he had invited some guy from work over to the apartment to watch the game. Some guy and his girlfriend. "She's an account executive for Merck," he said, grasping at commonality.

"But what if that pigeon is God?"

I waited for an answer but Evan didn't respond.

"I'm joking," I said as I rolled over.

"Of course you are," he said.

Lights off, sheets high, bolstered in a womb of anonymity, I said, "I'm not sure our relationship is salvageable."

To spite me, Evan responded, "This isn't a relationship."

"What is it, then?"

Uniquely facile with words, he responded with "Triage."

I visualized my ER rotation: stale rolls, torn silk, two off-duty police officers escorted the girl to the bathroom. Rape kit. Blood test. Social worker.

"You're not a nice person, Evan."

"You're right." He rolled over, pulled the covers up over his head. "I'm not."

When I was a resident, one of my first patients, a guy I would easily classify now as paranoid, refused to be photographed for fear that upon his death his image would wind up in a picture frame at an antique store.

We were taking a walk in the park—this was before digital photography and before I fully appreciated the necessity for doctor/patient boundaries. Just to be clear, there was nothing romantic between us. Still, I shouldn't have been taking a walk in the park with him.

"What scares you about that?" I asked.

"Adornment."

I patted his back with the palm of my hand. I didn't probe, ask what he meant, try to clarify, because I didn't need to. I understood.

Adornment.

A few weeks later, a brisk and bright autumn day, we went for another walk in the park. I had recently begun to knit and was wearing my first creation, a crimson scarf in a simple basket weave. I remember rubbing the palms of my hands together. I remember being happy.

My patient—Adam was his name—my patient Adam

was hungry, so we stopped at a street vendor. I'd been taking pictures of the foliage, and without thinking (Freud would undoubtedly argue that), snapped a picture of Adam buying a hot dog. Enraged, he threw the hot dog on the ground and lunged in my direction, saying, "Give me the camera."

I gave it to him.

Strangely enough, he didn't tear out the film or anything like that. He simply opened the back, exposing the negatives, and passed the camera back to me. I never heard from him again. He was, I swore, the last man who would ever leave me.

And he was.

I looked at Evan's legs. Muscular. Strong legs. Tree trunks. I wonder, still, how much of our relationship was based on his strength—on my needing a man who didn't waver. I mistook stubbornness for conviction, but I didn't understand that then. So I watched Evan sleep. Easy in. Easy out. A decade of my life.

I got out of bed, walked to the bathroom, and stood naked before my reflection. Pubic hair gray; eggs dry. It was too late. It was too late for me to be what I could have been or wanted to be. It was too late for me to merely become who I was and then wasn't before the doorbell rang, Mom made a noise that I still don't have the words for, and I understood that you weren't coming home. Which is all that really happened when it comes down to it. You left us, Dan. Mom and me. Me.

I studied myself in the mirror. So many years later, there I stood, still recovering.

"Pick one," you said.

"What am I picking?"

"Just pick." There were four crumpled pieces of paper in the palm of your hand.

I took one. "Now what?"

"Well, what does it say?"

"It says December 15, 2032."

"December 2032. Perfect."

"For what?"

You lit a joint. "Guess."

"You'll be turning sixty-four?"

"No, I'll be turning sixty-eight and you'll be sixty-six."

"And?"

"And on December 15, 2032, we're going to meet at the boat basin and we'll hop on a sailboat and—"

"Where are we going?"

"Into the sunset."

"Excuse me?"

"Like the expression. We'll sail off into the sunset and head toward heaven."

"You don't even believe in God?"

"Maybe I will by then. Have you ever met an old guy that doesn't believe in God?"

"But what about our families? We'll have families. I'll have a husband. You'll have a wife. We'll have children. Grandchildren."

"Your husband's more than welcome to join us and your kids will be grateful."

"Grateful?"

"Sure. Grateful that we never became a burden to them."

"Mom's not a burden."

"She's not?"

I smiled. "Fine. But what if we're feeling great?"

"Better to get out on top."

"But what if I'm not ready? What if I change my mind?"

"Then I guess you'll have to live without me."

"That's a mean thing to say."

"Is it? Why's it mean?"

"It feels like a threat."

"Nah. It just is what it is."

"Dan?"

"Yeah?"

"Your plan. Well, it doesn't make sense, because what happens if something happens to one of us before that date? Then what? I could get hit by a car or be in a plane crash or have a terminal illness. Then what? Don't you see? One of us might not even make it to that date."

"I'm just fucking with you, Suza. I wanted to see your reaction." I saw you pop something but I was too distracted to ask you what you were taking.

"My reaction?"

"Yeah, if you'd be willing to live without me. And now I know the answer."

"What's the answer, Daniel?"

"You'd be perfectly fine."

"You say the meanest things."

"What's mean about saying you'd be fine. It's good. I want you to know you'd be fine without me."

But let's say instead of rolling my eyes, I had brought you tea, tucked you beneath a quilt, waited at the end of your bed while you slept. If I were to have understood, have recognized what you were asking. If, instead of calling you crazy I said I was willing to go with you, would you have waited for me? Could I have saved you? Could I have? Because I would have, you know. I would have done anything—if I had understood, if I knew you were testing me—I would have climbed into that sailboat, Daniel. I would have met you there.

Happily.

Damn you, I thought as I buttoned my slacks, slipped on my shoes, grabbed my coat and hurried out the door into the city night.

Damn you, I thought as steam escaped through a pothole, an Asian man collected bottles, and I waited for the light to change.

Damn you, I thought as the little girl ran past, her legs so short her head was barely off the ground.

two

When I WAS A LITTLE GIRL, I WOULD SIT ON THE ROOF AND watch you spin around in circles. Arms in air. Palms toward sky. You turned and turned without ever falling. I should have recognized your balance was superior to my own. Instead, I stood, moved my body as you did, round and round, and quickly sank to the ground. You joined me there, leaned back onto your elbows, and smiled at me as I worried about how long the world would spin. Yours rotated on a singular axis, which I, for many years, mistook for purpose. Time spins until it stops spinning. That simple.

Later. Older. High. We watched the world spin without our having to move. And now, all these years later—even with distance—it is, still. Perspective, I've learned, is intrinsic to equilibrium. Happiness, on the other hand, is a sole operator. Denying you—click clock—until you become older than you ever thought capable. Your hands protruding from dark sheets drag the covers up over your head as you ache to remember and forget. Uncertain as to which would be a better outcome.

The pink morning light casts a glow across the ceiling. I check the time. It's 6:15 a.m. The train leaves at 8:15 a.m, so we have time. But not too much time. I swing my legs over the bed, grab my glasses. Today is your forty-fifth birthday. It's hard to believe we haven't seen each other in nearly twenty-eight years. I understand intellectually that twenty-eight years is a long time. I was a girl then. I'm a middle-aged woman now. But for some reason it doesn't feel like a long time ago and I don't feel old.

I guess there's some kind of cognitive dissonance at work, because there are still moments when I'd swear you're alive. Not whole, maybe, but pieces. On Halloween, for example, a three-foot-tall pirate—partial, I would soon discover, to Almond Joy bars—had your same bright and thoughtful eyes. I held out the candy bowl, he looked up at me, and in a flash, a split second between his hold-off and my go-ahead, you were alive.

What I've realized as I've gotten older is that time isn't, for both good and bad, a linear construct. The past beats beneath the present, threatening to unmask and reveal my regret to the world, or perhaps worse, to the forty-four-year-old woman who greets me every morning in the bathroom mirror. She too brushes her teeth, flosses twice a day, applies bleach strips to combat the inescapable decay. Cavities, receding gums, bone loss. The ability to delude oneself, and this I can validate from both professional and personal experience, is central to processing loss, yellow teeth enamel the least of it.

I keep two pictures beside my bed. One Margo sent a few weeks after your funeral. You're sitting on the bench at 149th, watching a subway car pass through the station. It has

"BERNARD IS KING" painted in huge orange and blue block letters in honor of the Knicks' legendary small forward. Just to the right, in smaller black letters, is your tag. "JAKYL." If you look closely, you can make out the shell toe of your Adidas resting atop a trashcan. What you can't see is that my feet are resting there too. Margo wrote "Memory lives forever" on the back of the photo, which is really not true. Memory lives only as long as the people who remember.

I spin.

I am spinning.

A rhinoceros dances on his tippy-toes. A porcupine eats ice cream and I wait for you to return to me. Your face—I can reach out and nearly touch it before you fade. It will never be that we will age together. You eternally seventeen. I try to figure out still. What I missed. Words I let pass, smells I didn't recognize, unfamiliar tastes and sounds. Each an opportunity I failed to seize. Each a possibility to save you. Although now, so many years, so many patients later, I am aware that treatment is not without consequence, death without promise, visions without meaning. And handholding is merely that.

You spin.

The foul-smelling summer envelops both moon and stars. You stand alone, nothing left to wish upon. But you insist. For what I'm still not sure. A sign of validation. A resuscitation of sorts? It doesn't occur to me to ask. You reach for my hands and I reach back—ours an unconditional covenant —until you break it, letting go.

You are spinning.

Lightning bugs illuminating Kodachrome.

Your teardrops, embedded in dust, have scattered into places I have more and more difficulty accessing. Around the corner—through the door—the third page in the navy photo album. Thirty-five-millimeter film. Auto exposure mode. There you are: orange towel, blue trunks, a slight smile and sunburn. There you are again, seagulls surrounding you, a bag of potato chips dipped in ketchup—what book is that you're reading?

And there I am. In the kitchen. A paper cup in chubby hands.

"Milk? Water? Apple juice?" Mom asks.

"Apple juice."

She returns from the fridge with a large glass bottle.

"Mommy, how much do you love me?"

We face each other. The smell of freshly cut grass itching at my nose. I mention this because we are away on vacation. It's a summer day, a beautiful summer day. The kind of day where people water flowers, paint houses, cut grass.

"How much do you love me?" I ask again.

"With my whole heart," she answers.

"Then what about Daniel and Daddy?"

"I love them with my whole heart too."

"How? How can you love all of us with your whole heart?"

"Well . . ." She takes a moment. "The heart isn't like a Dixie cup. It doesn't fill, it expands."

And then. Space and time a defy-able entity. You and I

are facing each other. You're sipping a milkshake through a paper straw. Daniel Seliger, age eight, sips milkshake through a paper straw, and when the straw softens, when he can no longer draw the vanilla through, he begins to cry.

I turn away. Memory is like this for me now. I can turn away from it. I repeat this thought out loud, as if the mere act of saying it, like an incantation, will transform the idea into reality. And because it's true. I can do this now.

Most of the time.

And yet it's the relentless tug of memory that brings me here. An early morning in December. Today was a day I always looked forward to. How you loved chocolate cake with marshmallow icing. I pull the sheets up. Fluff the pillows. Motion is not always action and action doesn't assure change. But there's no way to know that at seventeen, because at seventeen you still believe in the efficacy of revenge.

Michael Stewart deserves justice, Suza.

And you're going to accomplish this by spray-painting the side of a train?

It's so much more than that.

And it was. So much more than that.

In memory the concepts of space and time are rendered obsolete. You are alive. Your spirit lingering in stories. Of overcoming, triumph in fact and then not being able to overcome. Eventually the metaphysics won't matter because you will be returned to me. I to you.

And despite my rage at your stupidity, when you ask I'll allow you to take back my hand and lead me to the gathering. There we will dance in the absence of pain until morning or however long it takes for me to forgive you. Which will only happen when you accept how much I love, have always loved you. It's a crushing blow, the ferocity of that kind of love.

Dad died. Yes, I get that, more than anyone else in the world. His death was my loss too. Sugar Plum. Candy Bear. Sweetie Pie. I remember it. Miss it still. The view from high up on his shoulders.

But Dad fought to live. Round after round of chemo, bruised and battered, right hook followed by left. And when it became evident that there was no way he could win, he didn't retreat to his corner and wait for the bell. He faced down death, with the courage to look us in the eyes before looking away.

It's reductive and unfair actually to imply you didn't fight. You entrusted a notion: the bigger you were, the brighter, the more likely you were to be heard. If you were heard, you existed. If you existed, you could effect change. If you effect change, you matter. But moving trains pass by quickly, their messaging ephemeral, even to the working girl waiting on the platform. She appreciates your audacity, marvels even, yet remains oblivious to your plea.

You can't possibly know this because depression is an insidious disease. Robbing you of forethought, it makes you a reactive participant. Witnessing the world through the distorted prism of carnival glass leaves you feeling betrayed. The cruel nature of beauty. The unremitting groan of loss. You close your eyes and see him, cover your ears and hear. But that doesn't excuse your actions. You should have said good-bye, Dan. Or at the very least let me know you had to go.

The other photo I keep by my bed is a picture of my daughter. Mai arrived in an envelope. Staring at me from a rice paddy. I thought, *Pearl River department store.* I can get kimonos for her at Pearl River. I can replicate what's lost: bowls, chopsticks, rice cooker. How little I knew about being a mother. Sunday: NFL and Chinese takeout. How little I knew about anything really.

I walk across the hall and into Mai's room. She's sleeping on her back, arms and legs splayed, defenseless. I wonder if I ever sleep open to the world like that, if any adult does or if that's a sleeping position exclusive to little children. I sit down on the edge of Mai's bed, touch the tip of my finger to her cheek. She smiles, slowly opens her eyes, and upon seeing me reaches up for a hug. I wrap my arms around her waist, nuzzle my nose into her shoulder, smell her morning sweetness.

She's been mine for fifty-nine days.

Mine. It's still hard for me to process. Fifty-nine days ago I was just another passenger out of hundreds on just another plane out of thousands with just another life story out of millions. I'd like to think there was a steadiness in my eyes, Dan, the kind that brings to mind the look that women of the

Old West must have had—wise, determined, and above all honest about how hard anything worth doing is. I'd like to think if a person were to meet me, she'd see both the end of one difficult journey and the start of another in my eyes.

I've had these same eyes for many years—kind eyes, wouldn't you say? But they weren't as clear or focused. No, that's not true. They focused that way on others—my patients and friends—hardly ever on me. And not because I'm selfless. It was tactical, defense a trustworthy approach. I understood instinctually that people craved attention and at an early age began honing my conversation skills. As long as I asked the questions and listened to the answers, I would hardly be required to speak. There is always the hope that if you never say the words they might not be true.

But Jim's death showed me that I was running. I was running and had been running for so long now that I didn't know if walking was possible, which is cliché, the walk/run metaphor, but so is suicide when you think about it.

And so . . .

And so I picked a destination. The apex of a mountaintop. I ran there carrying, dragging the weight of a life unlived. I hauled her to the top, opened my mouth, and unleashed it all—the hate, loss, regret. I beckoned: God. Sky. Autumn in NYC.

"Love!" I heard. A response emanating from deep within a chasm. Was it you who said it? To let myself love?

I peered into the valley of hope. I peered into the valley of hope, a contaminated moat filled with alligators and razor blades, and I snubbed it. I said, "I can see from way up here. I can see the goldfish beneath you and they are dancing. They are having a party. They are celebrating. What? Their very existence perhaps. Down there, beneath your trompe l'oeil decay."

Detachment had turned out to be a reckless endeavor. An amateur ploy used to distract me from my very existence. But not anymore. It's been enough time. Too many years. Years that have left me with spoiled eggs and longing. Years where I've watched other people jump from right here—from this landing. Yes, I have witnessed other people jump from here, encouraged other people to jump from high up on this cliff—right into the abyss.

Smiling, are you? Smile. Keep smiling. There are goldfish beneath you. They are having a party, a goodbye party— throwing a goodbye party for a caterpillar named Delores— and so here I go. My arms extended. Here I go. Now is my time. You hear me? Now is my time.

I jumped and landed here, an early morning in mid-December. A little girl in speckled light. I rest her head on my lap, run my fingers through her silky hair. I jumped and landed here, a singular moment in time and space. Where I can say, even though you're dead, I am more than okay. I am happy.

The night before I left for Asia, Evan stopped by. We had spoken on the phone the week before—our apartment had sold, papers needed to be exchanged, releases signed. I hadn't seen him in several months, but he looked well. The madras shirt he was wearing was from a trip we took to New Orleans about five years ago. He brought a gift, a soft yellow bear with sweet eyes and a felt nose. "His name is Gregory." As I held Gregory in my arms, I thought, this bear is the kind of bear a little girl whispers to late at night. This bear, like my Winnie, is a secret keeper.

Evan gestured toward my suitcase. "So you're really going to do this? Fly to Cambodia, adopt some baby?" I conjured her face in the photograph—a little girl to love. As a shrink, I was aware that deciding to love this little girl was also a decision to love myself. That I was a little girl once. I sat on a swing, kicked my legs, and asked to be pushed higher, "Higher, Daddy!"

"Her name is Mai. She's four years old, almost five actually."

"You're really going to give up on us?"

Us? It was nearly comical. We had split up over a year and a half ago. There was no us. Still, I had the opportunity to play along. To enhance my narrative. I could have said, "You gave it up when you fucked that girl in Chicago." Or, "I'm sorry, don't you have a nearly two-year-old son?" Or I could have taken an entirely different approach and invited him to come with me: "Come with me, Ev. Let's be a family." Instead I covered his lips with two fingers and decided to fuck him until marginalized. A dick. An apartment. Twelve years of my life a Yankee fan.

And so,

Ear pressed against carpet.

I listened for a sonic boom.

A charge from the center of the earth.

Perhaps there is an existence of some sort other than ours.

A place, a destination, that all flesh travels to. In the ether. A juggernaut. A business trip. A two-year-old son in Chicago.

After, Evan, unaccustomed to grief, looked bewildered. "Love equals pain," he said as he buttoned his pants. Middle-aged men, I would posit, from both professional and personal experience, tend to pontificate. "It's a transaction."

I tried not to laugh

"The greater the love, the more costly the pain." Clue-less men are uniquely destructive—reclining, feet on table, flicker in hands, as the hours pass without notice.

"I miss you, Suze, in a way I've never missed anyone. Don't go to Cambodia. I told you we can have our own baby."

"I'm not mad anymore, Ev. I wanted a child and tomorrow I'm getting one."

Evan responded by asking me if I remembered to get riel, Cambodian money. "When you travel in a foreign country, it's smart to arrive with—"

"I have everything I need in my bag," I answered him, and I did: muscle relaxers, brain teasers, a book about the ramifications of abandonment. "Desertion," the author asserts, "creates a pathology of implication."

Evan sat down at the kitchen table and began tying his

shoes. "What's all this?" he asked. I gazed at the porcelain ballerina; next to it, a stuffed tiger and an autographed photo of Jerry Lewis. Newspaper ink stained the bride doll's dress. A heart-shaped box held baby teeth. I had removed them earlier in the day. One by one. Placed them on top of the table. The tea set was missing a teapot. The ceramic jar a lid.

A second box. A chair the size of my thumb. A stove that fits in the palm of my hand. A dollhouse—white with black shutters and a red door—as it should be. I set the little family up just as I had the last time. Mother, father, sister, brother. I dusted them slowly. With tissue.

There was the dress with embroidered flowers that I wore to elementary school graduation. A feather earring. A music box. What will these say to my little girl? I wondered. It was hard to even tell what they said to me anymore. Relics.

After Evan left, I unwrapped the last package, a jar of guitar picks and a 45 of "Don't Fear the Reaper." I realized then that too much time had passed to find meaning in any of it. Each item could be found on eBay. Mementos, boxed and secured, protected from the elements, become bookends. Solid and unassuming, they contain no information but rather hold it erect. How little I kept from childhood, how desperately I treasure.

Things will be different for my little girl. No circus tricks. I lifted the bride doll, face to face. Eye to eye. "Are you sure it's okay for me to do this?" I asked, and waited—

for only a moment—but for a moment I actually waited for permission.

I carried the tea set and then the dollhouse into her bedroom. I placed the tea set on a small child's table. I put the dollhouse high up in her closet. There was no reason to impose an antiquated version of home. No reason to play with what she didn't have.

In the morning I turned off every light in the house, unplugged the toaster, left a new message on my telephone answering machine. Then I locked my suitcase and walked out the door of my apartment, looking back one last time at the green vase on the kitchen table, my blue curtains and slipcovered sofa.

Fifty-nine days.

Through the OVAL WINDOW A CLOUDLESS SKY MASKED. TIME appeared to have stopped. Only stillness remained. Its quiet din offering consolation. I was alone. For now but not forever.

Fine.

Yet the possibility lingered. To be choked by pressurized air on a 747. I could have taken something but chose not to. I would sleep or not sleep. I picked at my cuticles, chewed gum, and stared out the window. "It's a long trip," the flight attendant said as she passed me a blanket and pillow. "Fifteen hours and fifty-five minutes from JFK to Hong Kong."

If only—

I counted on my fingers: June, July, August, September, October, November, fifteen hours from JFK to Hong Kong . . .

1983, 1984, 1985, 1986, 1987 . . .

If only that's all it was.

It was okay, though. There on that plane. Everything was okay. Which is why when the flight attendant asked me, "Is there anything you need?" I was able to respond, "I'm fine, thanks." Without feeling like a liar.

My hands challenged. Palm pressed against palm. Fingers coil, veins protrude—I look old, which bothers me. I look too old to mother a young child, but then again, I am old. Older than I was. Certainly older than I thought I'd be. Mai is turning five, so I would have been forty. Not an uncommon age to have a baby in the city. In fact, I see women like me all the time, middle-aged white women, chasing after their Asian toddlers.

About an hour before I left for the airport the phone rang. I let the machine answer. "You there, Suze?" I listened to Evan while pretending not to. I do that sometimes. Let myself think I am really cleaning the refrigerator. Windex works on spotted glass—

"I was hoping you'd pick up. I just wanted to say good luck."

—but not shattered.

So when my elbow slipped and the jar began to fall, I felt the need to reassure myself.

"Suze?"

It's only mustard, a small jar of mustard.

At ease talking to a machine, he continued. Wished me a safe trip: "Have a safe trip." I knelt to inspect the damage. The bottom had cracked. He took a breath. "It's a real noble thing you're doing." The jar remained whole.

Only then did I understand what he could never, that he—"Noble." I began to laugh. Am laughing still.

I couldn't sleep. Too many thoughts were racing through my head. I remember thinking that outside the window was my future. My future. I had never really thought in terms of a future. Distance from the past, yes. But not future.

I had plans. So many plans. As soon as we got home, we'd celebrate her birthday together, make up for the four we missed. We'd bake together. Every choice of cake she could imagine. But first I'd bring my little girl to the supermarket–to a giant Stop and Shop. I'd sit her down in the supermarket cart, we'd walk down each aisle, and whatever she pointed at I'd buy. "Oreos," I would say when she handed me the blue cardboard box. I'd toss it in the cart without checking the ingredients. Just that one time. Joy, one could argue, often tastes like high-fructose corn syrup.

I made my way down the aisle, past the sleeping passengers, and reminded myself that it didn't matter if I slept or didn't sleep. I entered the bathroom, bolted the door, splashed my face with water. And it was then that I saw her, Dan. The little girl I once was. She was smiling at me, and I thought, Little girls are resilient creatures, hiding in graveyards, under a white coat, behind the bathroom mirror of a 747. Every so often we dare ourselves to peek out and sometimes we even move forward, into the daylight—where the assassin has the open shot.

The airplane bathroom was small and dirty, being it was the end of a long flight, but I needed a moment to gather myself. I reached into my bag for my wallet, opened it and found you where I keep you. Just behind my MasterCard. I took your picture out. Look at you, high school graduation, navy cap and gown, just a boy really. Yet there was still so much I wanted to share with you—tears filled my eyes. "Can you be-lieve it, Dan?" I whispered, "I'm going to be a mom." I took a moment, kissed you, and then tucked you back into my wal-let. Just behind the MasterCard. Where I keep you.

"Cream or sugar?" The flight attendant asked, offering me coffee. "A little cream and a lot of sugar would be great." She smiled at me. I smiled back. It was morning in Phnom Penh. The seatbelt light came on, the captain's voice filling the cabin. "We are experiencing unusual turbulence. Please stay seated." It was only then that I was able to close my eyes—readying myself for sleep and descent and the sound of a child's voice calling, "Mommy."

"Mommy!" Mai's tugging at my shirt. I look down. "Oh my gosh, look at you." She's dressed herself in a pink tutu, pink sweater, pink polka-dot tights. She smiles, waiting for me to acknowledge the confection. I scoop her up into my arms, swing her through the air. Whee . . .

I carry her over to the kitchen table, plop her into a chair, and hand her "the breakfast menu." A little art project I made. Seven choices, each with a picture followed by its English name. A sunny-side-up egg. A bowl of cereal. Yogurt with berries. Toast with a pad of butter. Milk. Orange Juice. Water.

"What would you like for breakfast?" I speak slowly, ac-centuate each syllable. Then I read the transliteration. She takes a second, points her tiny pink painted fingernail.

"Egg," I say, "that's an egg." I hurry to the fridge and

grab an egg and hand it to her. She holds it in the palm of her hand. "Egg," I say again. She shapes her lips to match mine, opens and closes them as I do. She wavers but perseveres: "Ag."

"Yes!" She's so close. "This is an aaaayyyygg." I hurry back to the fridge, grab the butter. In a little while we'll bundle up and head out to the train station. I take a deep breath, put the pan on the stove, and turn the heat to medium.

The first thing I saw were her shoes—two little red clogs. The second was her face: porcelain skin, soft chin, hesitant almond-shaped eyes. "Hello," I pressed my palms together, bowed my head slightly, "Sous-dey." And then like a vampire I waited for a gesture, an invitation—the hint of a smile, curl of a finger—to enter the room. Thirteen months, clutching this little girl's picture against my chest, glancing at it between the pages of a book, invoking it in my dreams.

The mistress of the orphanage said something in Khmer. Mai hesitated, then reached into her shirt and pulled out her half of the small gold heart I'd sent her. I walked across the room, got on my knees, and we joined our halves. Without thinking, I wrapped my arms around her. "Anak kuchea anak mean sovotthephap," I whispered into her ear. Then again. "Anak kuchea anak mean sovotthephap." As I held her, tears dripped down my face. "You are safe."

It wasn't until that moment that I realized how lonely I had been.

Mai takes the fork in her left hand just the way I showed her. I pass her a piece of toast and she smiles. One day, not too long from now, we'll be able to sit across the table from each other and talk. I imagine we'll talk about everything a little girl talks about with her mom: mean girls, cute boys, last night's episode of her favorite television show. I'll test her on her spelling words, proofread her book reports, hold construction paper in place as she applies glitter.

She puts down her fork, wipes her mouth.

"All done?" I ask.

As she searches for the word, her little button nose moves up and down.

I help Mai onto the step stool; she washes her hands, then settles on the couch, ready for her morning fix. There are so many options now, so many shows to watch. We flip through the channels, settle on *Sesame Street*. Remember how frustrated I used to get when only Big Bird could see Mr. Snuffleupagus? It made no sense to me that something that was so big, that took up so much space, could be invisible to other people. But then, I think in many ways you were invisible to me. Not you, but part of you. There was something, right? Something trailing you around that I couldn't see? Hopelessness, was that it? Despair?

It wasn't loneliness. Between Margo, Mom, Ray, Tiny, and me, you were rarely alone. Not that you can't be lonely in a crowd of people, but I don't think it was that. It was fear,

I think; terror really. The persistent feeling of terror. Which is why you found comfort in risk, I guess. Hanging off the back of a moving train, tempting fate.

I was prone to withdrawal. Isolation provided comfort. Shades drawn. Air still. I was intact, I told myself, which was an improvement from broken. But inertia is a deceptive adversary.

You know Suze, rhythm has nothing and everything to do with time. Not timing.

First you surrender sight. Close your eyes and watch as your experiences play out against a black screen. Longing an effective substitute for living.

There you are. Clean hands, straight eyes.

You understand, right? Timing is something different all together.

A switchblade.

You don't need a man. To carve.

You don't want a kid. To bleed.

You don't need or want anything that you can hurt or that can hurt you. Think you're safe? Think again. Grief cannibalizes with virtue. Yet it is only in retrospect that I recognize my complicity.

I can SEE MYSELF AS I WAS THEN. JEANS, COWBOY BOOTS, your varsity jacket. My straight brown hair is tied back in a messy ponytail. Long bangs, the perfect length to catch tears, frame my face. Your blue duffel hangs from my shoulder. I reach into it and remove your old quilt. I shake it out, place it on the grass as if I'm preparing for a picnic. My movements are easy. I have clearly done this before. There is no tombstone, just me, you, a small patch of dirt. I run my finger along the earth before returning my attention to the duffel. I dig around, remove a red spiral notebook and flip through the pages until I find what I'm looking for.

"Things I forgot to ask:

"I forgot to ask why you didn't like egg in your fried rice and why you rooted for the Red Sox even though we had our own teams.

"I forgot to ask why you didn't meet me at the movies that time and why, when we were little and played hide-and-go-seek, you sometimes found me and other times turned on the television.

"I forgot to ask you how it was we began eating potato

chips with ketchup, who your favorite Beatle was, and if you remembered when Dad died how that little kid, the one who sold the lemonade in the courtyard—Bobby—how he said he saw Dad flying to heaven in a spaceship outside his kitchen window.

"I forgot to ask you what you thought of girls with short hair and if when I was little you were one of the people that agreed with Mom that my lips would be distorted if I played the clarinet and no boy would want to kiss me.

"I forgot to ask you what makes a girl sexy and if you can be sexy without being cool.

"I forgot to ask if you were Trans Am or Camaro, what you'd name a dog, and if you knew how much I really loved you."

My voice breaks then but I refuse to cry. "Sometimes I pretend you are still alive. Like the other day I stopped in that T-shirt store that you love—the one on Canal—and started fingering through the T-shirts. There's this cool new brand that you'd love. The T-shirts are super soft. They have these super cool graphics on them. I wanted you to have one so badly. So when the salesgirl said, 'What are you looking for?' I said, 'A gift for my brother.' She asked me to describe you. I said, 'He's around six feet tall, brown hair, brown eyes.'

"Cute?" she asked.

"Yeah—he's super cute."

"So what's the occasion?"

"He's turning eighteen this weekend."

"What about this one?"

"Oh, he'll love that."

"She rang me up, put the shirt in a gift box and tied it with a ribbon. As I was walking out the door, she tilted her head and said, 'Bring him in the next time.'

"I nodded my head and smiled at the sheer possibility. I couldn't help myself. It felt so good to be shopping for you, you know. The more I talked about you, the more alive you were. Anyway, this is the T-shirt we picked out. I hope you like it."

I reach into the bag and take out the box. From the present I watch myself open it. I hold up the shirt. "What do you think? Isn't the lightning bolt cool?" I put it down and begin digging through the bag again. "I was on such a high after getting you this, I stopped in the pharmacy to get you a bottle of Paco. A man asked me which perfume he should buy for his daughter who, he said, looks around my age. I sniffed both. Then I decided fathers, if he even was a father, shouldn't buy their daughters perfume. So I told him to go fuck himself. Go fuck yourself, I said, but not out loud. Out loud I suggested the small black bottle and he thanked me for what very clearly was an easy enough choice. After that I was done with shopping. Well almost, look what I brought you."

I take out a package of Twinkies. I open it, remove the small oval cakes and put a candle in each one. I light the candles and begin. "Happy Birthday"—I swallow—"to you. Happy birthday to you. Happy birthday dear Daniel"—I don't finish. Instead, I curl up next to you, ear pressed against earth, a thin layer of icing on birthday cake. So close I can nearly touch you, hear you. Just one last time. Humming would be fine. I would be satisfied to merely hear you hum.

I was, I know now, lying to myself. I didn't want to hear your voice. I wanted to die. I pulled the blanket up over my shoulders and closed my eyes. Maybe I'd get lucky and get run over by a bus, or an acorn might fall from a tree and hit my skull in such a way . . . or if the living are correct in their supposition and the afterlife is in fact binary, the devil's hench-man, bones in a cape, will grab me by the excess flesh of my arm and bite.

A watering pot. My blood saturates the earth. You emerge in the form of flowers. A nine-by-twelve patch of yellow daffodils. I throw myself on top of the bed of petals only to fall though a green screen. "Aha," the cameraman declares, "we nearly fooled you."

A car door closes. Another child at the playground. "The deceased was dead within seconds," the coroner reassured us. No pain. Which can't possibly be true, since you burned to death. I look up. An old man is walking across the grass. His body forms a C shape. A widower, is my first thought, but then maybe it's his sister or his mother he's visiting. Maybe a daughter. Maybe all of them are here.

I am cold but not too cold. Hungry but it can wait. I glance one last time at the old man. There is always someone who sees, I think, and close my eyes again.

There is always a witness.

Mom knocked on the door. "Ray's here."

"I don't want to see him."

"But he's here, honey."

"I understand, Mom. I told you I don't want to see him."

And I didn't. Wouldn't. One time, yes. He tried to explain himself.

"Daniel kept shouting at me to 'Go,' Suze. He said I had to make sure to get to you before the police did."

"And so you left?"

"I didn't want to."

"But you did. You ran away. Left him there to die."

"Suza, it wasn't like that. I didn't run away. I ran to you." Ray rested his hand on my shoulder, touch a human inclination, but I pulled away. The nature of grief is to rebuke charity and I was overcome with grief. So instead of accepting the kindness Ray offered I told him to, "Get the fuck out of my room. And don't come back."

But the nature of Ray is to come back. And so he always came back. Mom would crack open the door, "Ray's here, honey."

"I don't want to see him."

He'd linger, five-ten minutes. Maybe Mom would offer him a glass of milk and a couple cookies. Maybe a sandwich. Whatever snack she provided was enough encouragement for him to return. Just the mere acknowledgment that he existed.

This morning when she knocked on the door she said, "It's only me. Can I come in?" I didn't answer. She cracked open the door, waited. I didn't have the strength to fight. "Sure, Mom."

She sat down on the edge of the bed. "When your brother started school, he had a really hard time separating from Daddy and me. He was scared we wouldn't come back. I don't know why he had that fear. It's not like Daddy and I were jetting off to the Caribbean on weekends; we hardly went to the movies. But that was his fear. So separating at school was kind of a disaster." She crept closer. "On the first day of nursery school, Daniel cried and cried. 'Please don't go, Mommy. Daddy, please don't go.' So me, you, and Daddy waited outside the door. This went on for a month."

I rolled my eyes.

"No, really. I'm not exaggerating. Maybe two months. Daddy and I started alternating so at least one of us could have the morning to work. Anyway, it was my drop-off day and on the way to school we passed a busker with his guitar. He was hanging out on the corner signing an old Bill Haley song. 'See you later, alligator. After a while, crocodile.'"

"Mom, your voice."

She chuckled. "Fine, I won't sing. But Suza, it was the craziest thing. All of a sudden Dan got the biggest smile on his face and started dancing." Mom did this great imitation of you with your arms down by your side, moving about like a pogo stick. "So I gave Daniel some change to give the guy, Daniel dropped it into his hat, and we continued on to school.

"That morning when it was time to leave I braced myself, as I had been doing every morning, for the hysteria. I approached the block area to say goodbye, but instead of grabbing onto my leg he continued playing with the blocks. Without turning around, he said, 'See you later, alligator.'"

"I smiled and responded, 'After a while, crocodile,' and you and I went on our way."

I was still lying on my side, staring at the Bernard King poster that hung from your closet door.

"What's your point, Mom?"

"Even at four years old, your brother insisted on orchestrating the coming and going."

I said, "Well, he really didn't orchestrate it this time."

And she said, "Maybe you should rethink that. Ray, the two cops on duty. All three of them said he had more than enough time to jump."

"What are you trying to say, Mom?"

There is always a witness.

That was the morning of your eighteenth birthday. In less than a year I'd be as old as you were when you died. Every event after that would be independent of your experience of it. And before long, because time is funny like that, how quickly it passes, ten, fifteen years, before long I'll have lived more of my life with you dead than alive. Already, though, even that afternoon at the graveyard, when I heard the car door slam and saw the old man making his way across the cemetery, everything between us existed only as memory, which by construct is a misrepresentation of truth.

I was worried I wouldn't be able to differentiate what recollections were real and what were imagination. People can do that, you know. They can imagine something so much it becomes the truth. I couldn't imagine you back to life and was petrified that if I let go—if I unclenched my fist even just slightly—I'd lose part of you.

So I held on that afternoon like I had been holding on for days, on my side, curled up in a ball. Hours passed. Three, maybe four. Without opening my eyes I sensed his presence. "Why didn't he jump?" My voice was barely audible.

Ray sat down, wrapped his arms around me, letting me cry, which I did, on and off through the night until morning. "I'm here," he said. And then again. "I'm here." The morning moon set and the sun began to rise over the graveyard. An astonishing feat that it should rise.

Ray turned on the bathwater and waited for it to warm. As the tub filled he helped me take off my clothes. He held my arms up and lifted the sweatshirt I was wearing, your navy hoodie, over my head. Had me lean on his shoulder while he helped me out of my pants. Sat me on the top of the toilet and slipped off my socks. When the tub was full, he held me as I stepped in. I didn't lie back into the water like I usually did. I just sort of slumped over.

Ray trickled warm water down my back. When it was time, he lifted me up, wrapped me in a towel, helped me step out of the bath. He handed me a T-shirt and a pair of his boxers. "Here," he said, "I'll be right outside if you need anything." I took off my bra and underpants, changed into Ray's clothes, and opened the door.

I hadn't been in Ray's room for a long time but it looked just like the last time I'd been there. There was a worktable with an unfinished skateboard on it. Templates of board designs and a bunch of random *Thrasher* covers on the wall. His bedding was a worn beige and navy plaid.

"I'm sorry it's messy." Ray folded back the sheets.

"It's not, it's nice. Ray," I asked as I climbed into his bed, "what's going to happen to us?"

He pulled the blankets up to my shoulders. "We are going to be okay. Close your eyes, Suze."

I woke in a panic. "Ray?"

"I'm here, Suze."

I rolled over to face him. "Ray?"

He brushed my bangs off my face. "I'm here, Suze."

And then, most gently, he kissed me. On the forehead. Right between my eyes.

Ray was YOUR FRIEND FIRST. THE TWO OF YOU PASSING through the apartment, skateboards in hand. You would build ramps in the courtyard and I would judge. Give a 7.8. A 6.2.

"Suza, I'm your brother. I get the higher score." And then you would tickle me and Ray would laugh. He'd have dinner with us nearly every night. It was like that for most of our lives. Me, you, and Ray. A little family.

His dad would come home. Because he did that. Dragging chaos through the front door. He'd come home from tour all strung out and Ray would disappear for a few days. We would talk about it around the dinner table. Ray's seat empty.

"Sometimes passion exacts a price." Dad would say about Ray's dad.

"Then he shouldn't have become a father, Paul. We need to bring Ray dinner. You know that strung-out asshole isn't worried about feeding him." Mom would fill two plates and have us carry them down. Remember, Dan? How we'd press our ears against the door hoping to hear them. But it was always so quiet. So damn quiet in that apartment.

The first art award Ray received, New York City Middle School something or other, was for a sculpture of three clay daisies in a coffee can. Instead of water the flowers were fortified by pebbles. "It's called *Life Among Ruins*," he said.

Ruins.

Ray.

The three of us would sit up there on that roof trying to answer the big questions of the day: How did the Bee Gees get their voices so high? Who was hotter, Jaclyn Smith or Farrah Fawcett? Did Spinks finally get teeth? And of course there were the slightly more complex ones. Creation: Darwinism or God? Time: Which is longer, the future or the past? Life: What's the point if everything you love gets taken away? We never solved the question of creation or came up with the value of time. And the meaning of life? Eventually we decided that life's meaning—the "point"—didn't matter. "After all," you said, "even an empty pillow remains vigilant. The sheer possibility of being slept upon."

It stayed this way for quite some time. Years in fact. The three of us. Sometimes Tiny would join us. Margo. There was that kid from school, the bass player? George? Was his name George? Friends came and went. Some we really cared about. So it's not that we weren't affected by their absence, we were, but together we were fortification—Me, You and Ray—a barrier against—what in particular? Against all of it, really. The things we saw. The people we lost.

After you died, Ray and I became a sum of two. Which was mostly fine. Because we loved each other. In a way I've never loved, or allowed myself to be loved, by another man. Of course I didn't recognize the value in that. True unification a rarity. Although he did.

Ray was aware. Known and unknown. Fragility and consequence respectively. He nuzzled his nose into my lower back, kissed me. I pulled away. "Stop. My tush might smell." He brought me back, pinned my arms down over my head. All friendly. Warm. I tried to laugh. A coquettish giggle—to continue with this boy I loved, eager only, perhaps, to nibble at my cunt.

Stop.

I reached for the joint, lit it. "What's going to happen when you leave?"

When you leave? When you leave? What's going to happen when you leave?

He kissed my neck. My shoulder. "I'm not leaving."

"What would you call it then?"

"Art school."

"That's one I never heard before."

"That's not fair, Suze. It's a full ride."

I passed him the joint, glanced at his duffel.

"It's not fair to manipulate me like this, Suze."

I scooched back, drew my knees into my chest, and focused on my feet.

"Your toes look pretty."

He didn't want to fight and he was right. Why not have a nice night? I should have accepted the compliment and moved forward. But I didn't want nice. I wasn't looking for nice.

"Please," I said without emotion, "black polish is cliché."

"What do you want, babe? What more can I give you than my word?"

I don't answer.

"I'll be back in a couple of months."

"Maybe."

He gave me a playful punch to the arm. "What are you worried about?"

My eyes began to fill with tears. "Well, any which way you look at it, I'll be here waiting." A small act of kindness on my part.

"Perhaps." He smiled, passed me the joint. "You may decide to tour the Sahara."

"The Sahara?"

"One of those high school travel programs."

"You know I hate the heat." I put the joint out with my fingertips. Still I refused to look at him and continued to focus on my feet.

"People gravitate to all sorts of things they hate."

"True. I hate death and all I want to do is die."

"And I hate people who die and yet I love you."

"Love?"

"Yes, love. Of course love. Do I even need to say it? What more can I do to show you how much I love you, Suze?"

I wouldn't budge. "Let's see if you come back."

"You know"—he cupped my chin with his hand, looked

me in the eyes, all serious—"I'm going to miss getting high with you."

We began to kiss. Our last time. For now? Forever? He must have been thinking it too. He straightened my legs, moved his lips along my body. There was, I realized as his balls grazed my thighs, no way to mitigate the pain. The mistake was falling for him in the first place. I couldn't decide if it was funny or pathetic, me being so high and sad.

"What are you smiling about?" he asked as he kissed my navel. I should have told him that ours, an affair born from grief, can only die. That it is in fact already beginning to. But instead I closed my eyes and he continued to kiss me down there.

"I'm ready," I said.

He came up, brushed my hair off my forehead. Looked at me all serious. "You sure? You don't have to—"

"I'm sure."

So it happened. And I was no longer what people called a virgin.

Ray didn't go away to school. He gave up his scholarship, whatever future that may have amounted to, and stayed in the city with me. We got a little place on the Lower East Side. A tiny little walk-up on Ludlow. It was a stupid thing to do. Neither of us had any money but Ray said we'd figure it out. And we did. A single room free from construct. We painted the walls and ceiling yellow.

If the sun refused to shine. I would still be loving you.

A muddled light enters through the window. Our shadows, random and alive, manifestations of hope. Taking his in mine, I watch as his hands collapse, readying himself for ascension. He can still do this. Allow himself to rise and fall without the burden of consequence. Which is perhaps where the difference lies. Because I can't. Sometimes but not all. Yet my shadow appears as fluid as his. And so I remain optimistic. Day in. Day out. A hotplate. Two spoons.

When mountains crumble to the sea, there will still be you and me.

Years passed this way. Four. No, five. I would be graduating college in the spring and starting med school in September. Five years had passed, and, just like Ray said, we figured it out. For money, he painted people's apartments. He was good at it, appreciated the monotony. On Saturdays he took classes at the Art Institute and I worked, insignificant day jobs, waitressing, dog walking, that kind of thing.

I visited Mom, but not as often as I should have. It wasn't that she was morose. Quite the opposite. She was maniacally upbeat. Sometimes it was just too much to see her like that. I resented her for it. For finding redemption in a car salesman from Jersey. Which wasn't fair, because we were also getting better, Dan. Little by little Ray and I were beginning to heal.

Until we weren't.

Which happened because we were sloppy. That's not fair actually. Which happened because I was sloppy. We were unhappy because I was sloppy. What was it that Jim said?

"Hope makes a person sloppy and sloppy people forget things."

I was waiting for Ray at the diner around the corner from our apartment. A familiar table, third booth in on the left. I sipped my coffee, thin and slightly sour, as the cakes in the glass cabinet spun round.

The door chimed and I looked up hoping to see Ray. Instead I saw a woman standing in the doorway. A single light cast a warm glow on the top of her head, which was wrapped in a colorful scarf. It was clear that she was bald beneath that scarf, and she had no eyebrows. She scanned the room, smiling when she saw him. Then lifted the back of her hand to her cheek, a playful gesture, opening and closing it like the mouth of a finger puppet.

The man—husband, boyfriend, brother—responded appropriately. He walked over to greet her, his arms open, a kiss. He was taller than she. More than a foot. Her skin, the chalk white of a mime's, was her most distinctive feature. Yet she revealed, upon removing her jacket, very little of it.

They approached the neighboring booth with ease, genuine, possibly not. Which is no different from anyone in any situation, I guess, not when you stop to think about it. The ritual continued. He took her coat, pulled back her chair. She sat, placed the napkin, opened the menu. There were, as there always are, questions. Many. Some will be answered soon: grilled cheese or chicken fingers, Coke or iced tea. Some later: benign or malignant? Stage one, two, three, four?

There is no five.

The man and woman began talking about an episode of *The Phil Donahue Show*. Donahue interviewed a female cancer survivor who was told by doctors she had three weeks to live—and that was two years ago. She was on the show promoting her new tome, *Fistfuls of Leafy Greens*.

"Which," the woman said, "is the biggest bunch of crap I've ever read. Replace chemo with spinach? I wouldn't be sitting here if it weren't for modern medicine." She took a sip of water. "Although I might have my hair."

"Nadine." He smiled but it was obvious, from the way he said her name, not shyly so much as with an almost timid affection, that he was scared.

"I'm telling you Andy, it was the craziest thing. I sat on the couch with a bowl of ice cream in my lap and watched this animated skeletal figure go on and on about the healing power of beta carotene. She actually said, 'I am the picture of health.' And I thought, 'If I have to look like you, I'd rather be dead.' Oh, and by the way, he wears a toupee."

"Who?" her dining partner asked.

"Donahue! The lady at the wig store told me."

And with that the man punched his fist into the air. Because he could—wish bad things on TV talk show hosts, on all people that promulgate false hope.

Ray came up from behind and covered my eyes with his palms. "Guess who?" He sat down. "Let's go ice-skating." I gestured for him to listen. Which is something you used to love to do with me. Eavesdrop on other people's conversations.

The man and the woman had switched topics. They

were talking about a dinner party now. Seems the host introduced her to everyone at the party as "the cancer survivor." "'This is Nancy. The friend I was telling you about. The cancer survivor.'"

"How did you respond?"

"I laughed. I always laugh when I'm afraid."

The waiter put matching cheeseburgers in front of them. Then came over to our table, "Anything I can get you?" Again, so many ways to answer: chocolate cake, tiramisu, a head of wavy brown hair for the lady at the next table.

"Whatever you want, Ray, as long as it's something sweet."

Ray smiled. He even found my sweet tooth charming. "Do you have the Key lime pie today?" he asked the waiter.

"Sure do."

"A slice of that with two spoons."

"Be right back."

The tables in the diner were occupied by all kinds: men, women, boys, girls, cancer patients and mourners—each slurping and swallowing, clamoring to be heard as the cakes in the glass display went round and round. This, it suddenly occurred to me, is what people look like when they're waiting to die.

I should have explained this to Ray—that everywhere I looked, all I saw was death. Leafless trees lined the sidewalk, the sky was gray, the earth silent. I was three weeks pregnant with his baby. I should have told him that too. But Ray wanted to go ice-skating.

"What do you say, Suze? Let's go rent some skates and hit the ice."

And for the first time in a really long time, I didn't know how to answer. No, that's not true, Dan. Looking back, I knew how to answer. I didn't want to go ice-skating. I wanted to get an abortion. I wanted the microscopic vestige of life scraped out of me. I wanted to be cleansed of hope. I wanted to be free to run and hide and not have to put a smile on my face—not have to hold anyone's hand—especially across a sheet of ice where safety is measured in balance, and balance, you had already taught me, like so many things, is but an illusion.

So as you can see Dan, it turns out two is little protection against an onslaught of sorrow. And so it never could have worked out for Ray and me. But we tried. We tried for a long time and for a long time our love kept us afloat. I really do believe that. That we would have drowned if we didn't have each other. It kept us afloat until I, like you did, decided to discard it.

Mai and I HAIL A TAXI AT THE CORNER OF 101ST. THE DRIVER takes Broadway down to 96th, then turns right onto the West Side Highway. Outside the window a huge cargo ship is being guided down the Hudson by a tugboat. You had a plastic tugboat. Red. The tugboat had a yellow rope. Around the bathtub the tugboat went, delivering rubber duckies, bars of soap, various lost and deserted matchbox cars to safety. "This is what tugboats do," you explained. "They lead cargo ships hundreds of times their size to port." Somewhere out there a boy waited for a bike, a girl for an Easy Bake Oven, a woman for an imported turntable, and a dying man for a cure. "The tugboat," you argued, "is the superhero of boats." You maintained this position for quite some time. Even when others were into speed, you insisted on playing with your tugboat.

One time, a summer night—I remember this because you and I were muddy from playing in the park—I brought a small cardboard jewelry box into the bathtub. "Hello, Mr. Tugboat," I said, "I'm on my way to the jewelry store." The tugboat captain received this information with a smile, then proceeded to guide the small turquoise box through a sea of bubbles—but here's the thing, the cardboard box—although thoughtfully anchored on the far end of the tub—was now soggy. Its contents presumably damaged. This upset you much more than it upset me, to know that something could be safely delivered and yet broken.

It may have started at that moment, or maybe it just happened little by little over time, but somewhere along the way, your infatuation with the tugboat began to wane.

"They never go anywhere," you said.

It was many years later, more than ten, and you and I were no longer in the bathtub together but sitting on a rock facing the Hudson.

"Who never goes anywhere?"

"Tugboats. They never get to see the ocean."

We were eating chips and getting high for a change. "My God, everything's sad to you, Daniel. Five minutes ago you were distraught over a three-legged dog."

"What's sadder than a three-legged dog?"

"A two-legged one."

I look at the little girl sitting next to me, twenty thousand miles from home. She will always know the sound of her cry for help, the ache of her specific hunger. She will always know how it was she got the small scar on the lid of her upper left eye and what the touch of her mother's hand felt like. Yet she's here. A new world. A new life. A new woman's daughter.

They never go anywhere.

"No," I answer the echo in my head, and then I correct myself. "No, they don't, Dan, but does anyone?"

The taxi pulls to the curb. I pay the driver, take Mai's hand in my own, and together we march through the underground. Burnt rubber. Body odor. A dungeon perhaps.

No, not a dungeon.

This isn't a path to extermination. This is a train station. THIS (I hear in capital letters) IS A TRAIN STATION.

I know this because I've made this trip before.

Train. Taxi. Graveyard. Ten. Eleven. Twelve.

The last time, I was greeted—"greet" may not be the right word—by the sound of a man, the bellowing, that's better, last time I made this trip I was greeted by the bellowing of a man. A filthy man, he stood, socks no shoes, on a pile of newspapers. And from there, from on top of a paper soapbox, he addressed his audience. Three dogs. One big. Two small.

"You don't understand," he said, gazing into their plaintive eyes, "I am a bum. You have chosen to spend your life with a bum."

That despondent teenager, with her chewed-up fingernails, möbius ribbon of pink in jet-black hair, is now a woman. No longer do I need hair color to define myself. A mom in slacks and leather boots. My phone rings. "Hello, this is Dr. Seliger." A doctor. I should continue. I know this. I must continue moving forward. No reflecting. No taking in scenery. No getting confused. I give the pharmacist a prescription; drop the cell into my pocket, focus. The stairs are straight ahead, all twelve of them. I know how many we must descend in order to reach the platform because, and this must not be underappreciated, I have done this before.

Train. Taxi. Graveyard. Ten. Eleven. Twelve . . .

I glance at the tiled wall before descending. Only for a moment. I pause as if to acknowledge, to honor the fact that once, nearly thirty years ago, three nearly dead dogs stood looking to a defeated man for help. He knew it too, the man. Knew, as I did, what he was and was not capable of. If you announce it, if you tell them and they still refuse to believe you, are you guilty?

Stop.

I check myself in a pane of storefront glass. A toddler's concept of self. Again I am reminded that what I know about the biology of the mind provides little if any help to me as a human being. This is the dirty secret of my profession. Or perhaps it's just one of my many dirty secrets. Whatever it is, the fact remains. As much time as I've spent trying to understand the human mind, I haven't gained much perspective.

Twenty-eight years have passed since the night you died. Full decades consumed with ambient regret. First you. Always you . . . Although over time there were others. Smaller ones. Trips I should have taken. Women I might have enjoyed being friends with.

Ray.

Yes. I should have married Ray, had his babies, lived happily-ever-after, or if not happily-ever-after, I certainly should have given it a shot. But I couldn't afford to deviate from my neurological road map. So I held steadfast. Love only went in one direction. Away.

Which makes sense, right? It's safer to eliminate risk. You taught me that. And so I followed you. Not dissimilar really to how I always followed you.

Down the hall,

Remember the sounds that emanated from his room, Dan? A language all their own. Hope: a wail. Grief: a howl. Surrender: a moan. A barely audible moan.

through the front door,

I've witnessed it many times now. This unspoken dialect. The breath simply stops. A vestige of air. Possibly. But no tangible exchange. The world doesn't react. No matter how much you demand its attention.

into the car,

What gall. Really.

onto the grass,

To repudiate shame.

"Ashes to ashes."

"Dust to dust."

A wooden box buttressed by a steel mechanism. We tell ourselves we are managing. Even controlling.

watch it descend

Foolish. The fables we craft in order to survive. Dirt. Soil. Liquid bleach.

only to turn away.

"If you're going to face the music," some guy in a leather blazer—yes, leather—says into his cell phone, "may as well face it soon." I laugh at this. Look at me, standing there in the glass. Yes, you, Miss Twenty-Six-Years-Soon. I glance at Mai, entrusting somehow. Gregory secure in her arms.

The hows and whys can seem complicated, but it's pretty simple really. There are two options. There is laughing and there is death. And in between, for an infinitesimally short moment, if you decide to partake in the folly, there is life. I grab Mai's hand and we make our way over to the platform. The train pulls into the station, the doors slide open and we enter.

I'm a FIFTEEN-YEAR-OLD IN PAT BENATAR BLACK AND BIKER boots. And there you are, tall, thin, fragile-looking. Your shaggy hair frames your face. It's the end of summer, so you have some color. There you are, sitting on the edge of your bed, cords and a Run-D.M.C. T-shirt, waiting for me to return. Which I do. Two plates. One under each arm. A jar of peanut butter in my right hand. Jelly in my left. You smile when you see me. I smile back. A bag of Wonder Bread clenched between my teeth. I spread out a towel. I make us a picnic. And I pretend, fact or fiction, that it's another Saturday night in September. And that we are fine.

I smooth peanut butter on one piece of toast, jelly on another. I face them toward each other and as I press them together I hear them "kiss" and then I hear our father's voice say, "When Peanut met Jelly, it was love at first sight." Dad's not sick yet. He's healthy and young and has a mustache. He peels back the corner of his sandwich; you and I peel back the corners of ours. "Make a wish," he says. Dad closes his eyes, takes a breath, and whispers his wish between two slices of bread. You and I close our eyes and whisper our wishes just like he does. And then just like that he's gone again.

I lift the corner of my sandwich and gesture for you to do the same. "Really?" An incredulous grin. I hold firm. "Really?" You shrug your shoulders, lift the corner of your PBJ, and together we pray to a god named Skippy.

Mai is looking out the window, a stuffed bear named Gregory on her lap. Everything she passes is new: asphalt rooftops linked by electrical wires, open-faced satellite dishes beckoning a winter sky. Mai pulls my shirt and points at a lone antenna standing defiantly erect. She pulls again. Language will come, I tell myself. Words will come.

I grab the notebook and pen from my bag and make five short lines, left to right, then a longer one up to down. "That's an antenna," I say. She nods her head. I begin to draw a simple stick figure: two legs, two arms, a circle head. There he goes, leaping from this sky wire of my creation in order to people a square TV. "TV," I say, hoping she understands.

Mai presses the top of her tongue to the roof of her mouth. "Tee." She takes a breath. "Vee."

"Yes." I nod my head and smile. "TV."

This could, in another circumstance, become a lesson on obsolescence: "That's an analog antenna, honey. TV works on digital frequency now, so we don't use them anymore."

I might use this to explain that time passes regardless of how tall you stand or tightly you grip. Technology advances and one day, despite years of protest, she will go hunting for her biological parents. And she will find them, a scribbled name, a strand of hair, a global DNA database. And when she finds them, she can ask how they could leave her on a doorstep.

How they could promise to be right back and not return.

Twenty-eight years, a day, a moment, a life.

"What do you wish for, Dan? Like do you always make the same wish or do you wish for different things?"

You didn't answer. Didn't have to. I phrased it wrong. I should have asked for something specific. An object, not a yearning.

"Did you ever wish for a toy or something?"

You took a bite. "Remember when I wanted that Stingray with the banana seat? I ate, like, three of these a day."

I swallow, then smile, because of course I remember.

And now I'm on the bike. I'm sitting between the handlebars. Legs out. We are at the shore. We are visiting friends. I don't like the feeling. I don't like having no control, so I scream, "Stop! Please stop, Daniel," which you do because you always stopped when I said stop.

And now you're helping me onto my own bike. You lower the seat. Pad the pedals with newspaper. You talk balance and counterbalance. You push me until I can do it on my own. One foot followed by the other.

And now I'm pedaling next to you. Just one summer later. Dad is dead. But we are, we think at that moment, just then, with the wind blowing back our hair, getting better.

"What about you? What did you wish for?" you asked.

I said, "For nothing to happen to you," but it was too late. You raised the volume on the television. *"Thousands of people are holding a vigil tonight for the slain graffiti artist Michael*

Stewart. The twenty-five-year-old was taken into police custody on September 15. Officers say they stopped him for writing graffiti on subway walls after 2 a.m., and that he resisted arrest. Family members say he was on his way home to Clinton Hill after work and the cops beat him to death. Along with Stewart's friends and community activists, they're accusing the police department of brutality, pointing out that eleven officers were involved in the dispute, all of them white. The official cause of death is cardiac arrest."

The segment segues into a report on gas prices. You turn off the TV. "All the guy was doing was trying to make something beautiful. I gotta go."

"Please can I come with you?"

"No. Vandal squad's out for blood. The city is about to blow."

I roll my eyes. "Please, it's not about to blow."

"You don't know that and I can't risk you getting caught up in a riot or something."

"So I'm just supposed to sit here waiting while you vandalize another subway car?"

"I wouldn't call it vandalism."

"What would you call it then?"

"A tribute. Michael Stewart lost his life protecting the First Amendment. Freedom of speech is an inalienable right of every—"

"Michael Stewart defaced public property."

"Exactly. Public. And the cops killed him for it."

"Cops killed him 'cause he was black and they had a bad night and that's terrible. Really, Daniel. That's really terrible.

All I'm saying is Michael Stewart didn't make a selfless choice, didn't throw himself in front of a train to save a child or pull a little old lady out from the middle of the street and nearly miss being hit by a bus. He didn't tag the subway in an effort to protect the First Amendment. He didn't give his life—it was taken from him and that's horrible but not heroic."

You opened your closet, reached under your jeans, and pulled out an old wooden toy box filled with bombing supplies. You grabbed a can of Krylon Spanish Brown and tossed it into a navy gym bag. You took a sheet of paper out of your back pocket and unfolded it. You checked the blueprint against the paint colors: Mint Green, Flat Black, Avocado, Teal, Regal Blue, School Bus Yellow, Baby Blue, two cans of Titanium White. One after another, all the colors on the list were transferred. You tossed in a baggie of caps and some markers. There is no peace. Or glitter sky. Just an old wooden toy box, formerly the home of superheroes and action figures.

I pressed the image against my forehead and begged in an effort to conjure. A toy Evel Knievel on a toy motorcycle, a stack of Mom's eight-track tapes. You turned the crank, blew a strawberry-scented bubble, and we watched Evel fly over *Harvest* and *Houses of the Holy* only to crash into *Astral Weeks*. You were nine years old, so you laughed. I was your little sister, so I laughed too.

You dropped the gym bag on your bed, put a couple T-shirts between the paint cans so they wouldn't clang. You surveyed the room to make sure you hadn't forgotten anything. You grabbed the box cutter and a pack of Life Savers off your desk. Your motions were fluid. All set to go. A modern-day warrior. An aerosol can.

"Tell me who you think is heroic then, Suze. If Michael Stewart isn't heroic, who's heroic?"

"Firemen are heroic."

"That's too easy—someone you know. Want one?" You offer me a Life Saver and I take one.

"You don't know Michael Stewart."

"That's where you're wrong, Suze. I never met the guy but I know him. We're part of the same community. We're all trying to say the same thing."

"What are you trying to say, Daniel?"

"That we are alive. That we have the right to be heard."

I know then that I have lost. That there is nothing more I can do to keep you in the room. But I try anyway. My arms stretch wide to block the door. "Please don't go, Daniel. Please don't—"

You press stop, pull the headphones down around your ears. You put the palms of your hands on my shoulders. You promise you'll be okay. You say, "I'll be okay, Suze. I promise." You don't look at me. Instead, you kiss my forehead. A paternalistic undertaking. I respond, tears falling from eyes, by wiping my nose.

Mai's fallen asleep on my lap. I adjust her head, place the palm of my hand on her chest, feel it rise, then fall, then rise again. We will be arriving in Farmingdale in twenty minutes. Until then I will be satisfied to feel her breathe.

An aerial view.

I am on an operating table. Naked except for an old pair of red cowboy boots and a denim skirt. There is a huge gash down the center of my chest, exposing an empty cavity. My heart is on the rolling cart just to the right of me. Fastened to a monitor, it beats in unison with a 45 record.

I can't make out the words to the song.

A man in surgeon's blues picks something out of my heart with a pair of tweezers and drops it into a metal bowl.

Ding—

A second time, *ding*—

"What are you looking for?" I ask.

ding—

"Baby teeth," he answers, all matter-of-fact, as if extracting baby teeth from a live heart were an everyday occurrence. His voice vaguely familiar.

"Do I know you?" I ask. He doesn't turn around. Doesn't answer. Instead he cups the beating organ in one hand and fastens it to a set of yellow pulleys with the other. The apparatus eerily similar to a plastic Lego crane.

I try to ignore this. The sense of play. And focus on the

heartbeat. The man in blue locates a sound, says "It's beating" to a form in the distance. But I can't hear my heartbeat. Or the song. Only white noise. Needle scratching vinyl. And a response from the man in the distance: "A heartbeat is a positive sign."

A box of bakery cookies is resting just to the left of the scalpel. The man in blue unties the bow, opens the box, and eats one, a butter cookie dipped in chocolate. He secures the red and white bakery twine to the eraser end of a sharpened yellow pencil. Enjoys another cookie, a chocolate one with rainbow sprinkles. He doesn't wipe the crumbs from his lower lip or rinse his hands. He simply brings the right side of my chest to meet the left and begins to weave the pencil into one side of my flesh, then up and out through the other.

If chance and purpose joined hands at the waist, the discovery of movable objects from the past would bear down hard against the enveloping sky but not puncture it.

"Die," I heard, or was it "dance"?

Outside, looking in, even a moon questions its purpose. Time always defeats need, which is unfair. Especially to a little girl: black leotard, bloodshot eyes. "To the left. To the left," the teacher shouted.

"Okay," she responded, moving to the right, which is after all someone else's left. But you aren't that someone else now, are you?

Memory. Masterful and alive. Gases everything. Speculation. Pride. It's this way, not that.

Fine.

A snapshot mutates. A boy spits sunflower seeds out a school bus window. Kicks a bird's nest off the fire escape. Plucks stars from an angry sky. Afternoon entertainment is okay, I think. My toothless heart sprouting wings only to flutter beneath a freshly sealed wound. "Abort the mission. This is flight command. Do you read me? Abort the mission."

Ray was sleeping. Soon he'd wipe the crust out of the corners of his eyes, reach across the bed for me—we had a mattress now—"Suze?" If I didn't answer he'd sleep a little longer, maybe throw on his boxers and smoke a cigarette on the fire escape. Still an early riser, I'd head out first thing, buy the paper and coffee. He'd wait out there for me. Shout, "Hey, sexy," as I crossed the street. And I'd look up at him all handsome and strong.

If he called my name and I answered, it would be from the foot of the bed. I'd be sipping coffee, reading a medical journal, maybe just watching him sleep. "Morning, babe." He'd reach for me and I'd fold into him. When time permitted, an easy morning fuck.

But on this morning, instead of scampering across the street or saying "Hey, Babe," he'd find a note taped to the bathroom mirror. I remember thinking, but only after, that I was no different than you. No better. But at the time, I told myself Ray would be okay. After all, I had absolved him.

Dear Ray,
This is not your fault.
As if absolution is something that can be possessed,
You offered me your everything.
let alone bestowed.

So I watched him sleep for a little while longer. His thick black eyelashes would flicker every so often. His mind held captive to a world he had no more or less control over than this one. It wasn't the flickering of Ray's eyelashes or his open mouth that gave me pause but his shoulders.

Solid. Broad. Powerless.

I touched his shoulder blade one last time. A slight touch. The tip of my finger against familiar skin. And he said, still heavy with sleep, "I love you." And I said, which wasn't a lie, "I love you too."

And I knew. I knew that I was breaking him, Dan. I knew I was breaking him and breaking him in such a way that he could never be repaired. Never become whole and yet I did it. A tap on the shoulder, an "I love you too," on a morning like any other morning. I walked out of the building into the murky air. Still and thick. A small duffel hanging off my shoulder. It's amazing how little we actually need in order to survive, isn't it? I glanced back at the window and, in a cruel fantasy, imagined seeing Ray climb out onto the fire escape. But he was a late sleeper. I would already be well on my way.

My actions weren't entirely unprovoked. The future is a cunning adversary. It beguiles the present with the possibility of discovery. So it doesn't happen again. That particular sorrow. Why not? I thought. They cured polio, didn't they? It was an opportunity to learn from a pioneer in the field. So I moved to the Midwest and devoted myself to studying the effects of electricity on the mind. Odd choice, I know, for the little girl terrified of lightning.

God's wrath became my talisman. More specifically the notion that the same bolt of light that penetrates a blackened sky, when channeled into energy—a key attached to a kite— had the potential to eradicate sadness. I held on to it, committed to making it my life's work, all the while telling myself that my interest in psychiatry had nothing to do with you. But of course it did. It had everything.

I could, and for many years I did, excuse what I did— not excuse exactly but justify leaving Ray by blaming my actions on grief. On Dad and you having died. And that wasn't dishonest. In fact, I could argue that every choice I've made since the day you died was a response to grief.

But grief—and you don't realize this until later, if you realize it at all—is a quicksand emotion. The better you become at the art of rationalizing your behavior, the more certain you are to sink.

Whatever the motivating factor, the specific ratio of grief to cruelty is immaterial. I left Ray, without warning, as he slept. Out of sight isn't out of mind but it's out of the line of vision, which is something. Because you can keep quite busy like this. Moving forward.

It was a two-and-a-half-hour drive, according to Map-Quest. Three with traffic. So I could what? What was the point of driving up there? To confront my sorrow like the TV talk shows suggest? It's all nonsense. I knew that. And I also knew it wasn't.

Years ago I dated a surgeon named Philip. Nice enough guy. Met him on the cafeteria food line. He went with the "You look like a woman who deserves better than this" approach. A couple of nights later we had dinner at a Japanese place down the street from the hospital. He drank sake and talked about himself, which made it easy. There was racquet-ball, an upcoming conference in New Mexico, an orthopedist brother in Texas.

It wasn't until he mentioned having lost a patient earlier in the week that I actually focused. "Nine-year-old kid says, 'See ya later, Ma,' heads out on his bike, turns the street corner, and gets hit by a car not twenty yards from his house. The driver wasn't speeding or checking texts. There was no alcohol in her system. She was simply making her way home from work, a route she'd taken day in, day out for years."

The waiter placed a bowl of edamame on the table. Philip brought a bean to his mouth. "Kid wasn't wearing a helmet." He put the edamame shell in the dish, reached for another. "Didn't matter, though. His chest was crushed. Nothing I could do."

"You're only human. Can't save everyone."

"Yeah," he said, "I hate to be reminded of that. And the boy's mom wasn't, not that it's ever easy but she went at me, pounding her fists. I caught her forearms and held her until a nurse shot her with a sedative. That's the hardest job in medicine. To look into a mother's eyes and tell her that there was nothing you could do. That you couldn't save her kid."

"I don't think you can survive that. The death of a child."

"All depends on how good a storyteller you are." Philip poured me another glass of sake. "The boy's parents will have to figure out a way to give his death meaning. Start a charity in the kid's name. Lobby for more comprehensive helmet laws. You're a shrink. You know this better than anyone. Surviving grief requires relentless negotiation with narrative."

"Doesn't Jesus control that narrative?"

Philip took another sip of sake. "If you're lucky enough to have faith."

"By your tone I assume you're not a Catholic."

Philip smiled.

"Neither am I." I finished what was left of my sake. "Let's talk movies. What's your favorite movie, Phil?"

"Philip. Phil doesn't inspire the same confidence as Philip. You want a surgeon named Philip."

"Got it." I had successfully changed the conversation. "Okay, Philip, what's your favorite movie?"

By the end of dinner Philip probably thought, "There's possibility here." Knicks. Carson. *Godfather 1*. Many a union has been formed around less than that. So we skipped dessert and headed back to his place. The sex was as you might expect. Surgeon sex. His gilded dick mine for the sucking, which works for a flagellant like me. Head bowed in shame. But he was a nice enough guy; we carried on that way for quite some time. Dinner, then fucking. An occasional movie.

What I knew, and what Surgeon Phil knew as well for that matter, is that there's no sufficient story. Momentary distraction, yes. Seasonal even. Virgin snow. A crocus insisting on daylight. Lovely. But anguish can't be conquered. So memory keepers beware: there are no annotations. Time alters, and what was becomes something else, and with more time it becomes something else yet again.

But here's the thing, Dan, no matter how they frame it. No matter what that dad and mom tell themselves in order to survive the seconds, hours, minutes of every day: The dad will never share another bowl of Frosted Flakes with his son, have a catch, teach him to shave. And the mom won't ever take him for sneakers, watch any more slam dunk contests with him, bake his favorite cake. The mom and dad will never be able to share a laugh with him, hold him, even fight with him. The boy is dead. Their son is dead. As you're dead. Dad's dead. And now even Mom.

I was a girl. I didn't know that then, that twenty-four was a girl still. What I did know is that I had to leave. I was certain. If I had known then what I know now, I'd have known that certainty exists to serve a child's pleasure. I am strong enough to make it across the monkey bars, smart enough to figure out that problem set, kind enough to desert you.

I bore right as the GPS suggested. Pulled off the exit and made my way down the road. Hills. Trees and sky. In the distance smoke rose from a giant smokestack. A warning sign? A declaration? Behind it the shadow of a green hill. I pulled over to the side of the road. 1.2 miles. Estimated time: 2 minutes, 54 seconds.

Of all things, I started worrying about my outfit. I had thought about wearing the denim jacket Ray made me. Wearing it as a lark almost. A way to ease the tension. Why not, I mean isn't this why I've kept it in my closet all these years? For the right moment?

I would ring the bell, he would answer. It would be awkward. But then he'd remember his manners and invite me into his home, gesture for me to go ahead into the living room. When I passed by him, he would see the back of the jacket and remember. "Benatar?. . . Really? Still?" and we would be transported to the world we once inhabited, where the only thing that he questioned was my taste in music.

But that might not happen. Ray might not even let me into his home. It was a random Tuesday morning in March. I was returning the same way I left. Without notice, on my terms. The arrogance in that. No, that's not fair. It wasn't arrogance as much as a narcissistic desperation. I needed help. Yes, two, it turns out, is little protection against an onslaught of sorrow, but for a long time his love kept me afloat. Which I never thanked him properly for. And for which I never apologized.

I turned right onto Holly and took that to Long Hill,

where I made a left. And counted. Eight, nine, ten. I stopped my car across the street from his home. A modest farmhouse. The siding white. The shutters green. A woman, younger than me but not young, hurried from the car. The front door opened and he stepped out. A man now. Solid and broad as I left him. But sturdier somehow. As if somewhere along the way he had been given permission to stand straighter. It's funny, Dan, I didn't cry when I saw him. I smiled at his very existence perhaps. Gray t-shirt. Beat up sweats. It's impossible to overstate the advantage of being alive.

Ray handed the woman a bag, her lunch maybe, then a quick kiss for the road. I thought, Okay, she'll leave and I'll cross the street, make my way up the path, ring the bell. About fifteen steps. Fifteen steps to get from the driver's seat to his front door. Every step. A heartbeat. A breath. A blink of the eye. If you ring the bell and he doesn't answer, doesn't recognize, doesn't want to see.

Oh, wait—a little boy? Where did he come from? He darted across the lawn and hopped into the backseat. The woman passed him the bag—ah, the lunch is for him—then she buckled him into his car seat and closed the door.

The boy, four maybe, possibly five, poked his arm out the open window. "Bye, Dad." One last goodbye as the engine growled and she reversed. Unaware of the direction between then and now. God's olive branch of sorts. "Bye, Daddy." I was too late. Goodbye.

I waited. Twenty minutes maybe. Then began making my way toward his front door. Every step supposition. A heartbeat. A breath. A blink of the eye.

The last time was by chance. I was standing at the entrance to the farmers' market, scanning the list of vendors. I had gone there to buy a flowering plant for my new apartment. Some apples. Perhaps a jam. "Suza?"

It had been seven years since I walked out on him, yet thirty-something Ray looked eerily similar to twenty-something Ray and even middle school Ray. More rugged for sure but his hair was still thick and black, his honey eyes sweet and slow. It's not that they were untouched. They had traveled. Seen. Yet they were welcoming somehow. To me. To the world in general.

"Hey, Ray." It took both of us a moment to collect ourselves. But once we did, it was surprisingly easy. We walked around for a little bit. Made small talk. Yes, it's been a long time. Yes, the produce is fresh. Yes, I'm back for good.

"What about you, Ray?"

"I'm moving upstate on Monday. My dad died, so there's not much keeping me here anymore."

"I'm sorry," I said. "I would have called but . . ."

"Don't worry about it. You didn't know."

But I could have. Twice a year I came home to visit Mom. If I were a nice person, I might have called him, we could have met up for coffee. But I didn't call. Not once. I did return his calls. Early on. I explained it as best I could. Why I felt I needed to leave. That it was nothing that he did. I even told him that I would never love anyone like I loved him. And it was true. I never would and never have.

"What did he die from?"

"Alzheimer's." Which is a perfect way to die for a junkie. No plea for mercy, just the vacant whine of faith. "By the end he spent his days eating tubs of vanilla ice cream and wearing diapers. There were moments I got a little satisfaction, watching him shit himself. That's a terrible thing to say."

"No, not terrible, Ray. He was a cruel man."

"Yeah. But he was my father."

It was only then that I realized the magnitude of my cruelty. Because that's what it was, Dan. What I did wasn't mean, it was cruel.

"Anyway, I figure it's as good a time as any. To get out of the city. Head upstate. Find myself some trees and sky." And then he said, "You look good, Suze."

We went back to his place. A fifth-floor walk-up in Greenwich Village. Ray was making custom skateboards for a living. They were hanging from the walls, face out, like electric guitars. He was selling them at a few board shops and through the Internet. They featured Ray's signature bold colors but his artwork was more refined. Instinctual cool. Some had a hint of the political to them but most of them relied on visual incongruities. They were simply awesome. "These are awesome, Ray."

He laughed. "That whole big fancy education and the best you could come up with was 'awesome.'" He said this affectionately. The boy he'd been a man now. Somehow he managed to continue to live by a code. His code. To love purely. To believe implicitly.

Because. Despite.

I kissed him. First his lips. Tentatively. Then his neck, just behind his right ear. I ran my fingertips over the scar on his rib cage, gently squeezed his nipple. Every touch tainted with remorse. So that when he finally entered, I wasn't welcoming him but climbing aboard.

After, he walked me to the train and waited with me on the platform. "What do you think Daniel would have thought of cell phones?" I gestured to a woman on her phone. It was the first time I had mentioned your name. And looking back, it was a cheat. A way to have you enter the conversation without my having to take responsibility for guiding it there.

"He'd be like, 'I don't answer the phone at home. Why would I want to speak on the street?' Or it would become some political statement, 'Beepers are for the proletariat.'"

"'Cell phones are for suits.'"

"That's exactly what he'd say. 'Cell phones are for suits.'"

We both smiled and then kind of drifted off in thought.

"I worry about you, you know?"

"You'd think by now you'd have realized what a waste of time that is."

"It's impossible to overlook the extent to which civilization is built upon a renunciation of instinct," he said.

Problem is same guy said, "Time spent with cats is never wasted."

Ray put his arm over my shoulder.

"It's starting to feel like a long time ago," I said, "like the New York we grew up in is gone."

He pulled me close. "Suze? Do you remember, it was a few weeks, maybe two weeks before Daniel died, and we were at Margo's parents' place on Fire Island. You wanted to build a sandcastle, so we all took turns helping you.

It was this amazing castle with a moat and a bridge. Later in the afternoon Dan said, 'Susa, you should stop. The tide is coming in,' and you looked up at him and said, 'Oh, I know.' But instead of packing up for the day, you continued to make a pretty seashell path. I remember looking and you lining up those small white seashells and knowing that I loved you—that I wanted to spend the rest of my life with you because you continued to work on that sandcastle knowing it would be destroyed—that there would be no trace of it. I don't know if you remember—do you remember?"

"I remember that sandcastle."

"After dinner we went back to the beach to hang out. The sky had darkened. The summer was quickly coming to an end. And your sandcastle was gone. Margo felt really bad about it. She kept saying, 'We should have taken a picture. We should have taken a picture.' I thought Tiny was going to fucking murder her. But you weren't upset. You said, 'Margo, just because you can't see it doesn't mean it doesn't exist.'"

I bit my lip, trying not to cry. Ray gently cupped my face in his hands, obliging me to look at him in the eyes. "He's still here, Suze. In those tunnels, on those benches, under that tin. Just because you can't see him doesn't mean he's not here."

The express rolled through the station, the local just behind it. The doors opened, Ray handed me an envelope, I glanced at it. Simple and white. And then he kissed me on my forehead. Right between my eyes like he always had.

From the train I watched him become smaller and smaller until he vanished. I took a seat, opened the envelope. Inside was a key, attached to the key was a small tag. On one side of the tag there was an address for "87 Willow Road. Beacon, NY." On the other side of the tag Ray had drawn a simple square house with a triangle roof. The chimney had smoke coming out of it. The front door was red. To the right of the house was a puffy green tree. To the left a row of yellow flowers. Above the house flew a bird. Attached to the bird was a banner that said, "Come when you're ready. I'll be here waiting for you."

It was the last time I let myself cry over you, Dan. And I didn't cry because I missed you. I cried for what you had stolen from me. A simple square house with a triangle roof.

A puffy green tree. A row of yellow flowers. I knew at that moment I would never make it to that house.

I rang the bell.

Ray shouted, "Kerry, what did you forget?" I could hear the smile in his voice and began to panic. I thought I had played through all the scenarios, anger, surprise, indifference. But it never occurred to me that Ray would be disappointed. I didn't think I could endure that—to not be an object of his desire. He opened the door, but before our eyes could meet I did what I was best at. I ran.

"Susa?"

I could hear him calling my name, "Suza, wait." His voice was muffled, which disoriented me. My legs gave out and I sank to the grass. Cloudy headed. I pulled my knees to my chest and began rocking back and forth. Ray sat down next to me. Winded. We didn't say anything for a while. We just sat there trying to catch our breath.

A car slowed, then passed.

Ray brushed dirt off the soles of his feet.

"You're not wearing shoes?"

"I hadn't planned on taking a run this morning."

Another moment of quiet.

"I'm so sorry. I should have called. I don't know what I was thinking. When I got here and I saw—I didn't know you had a family. I wouldn't have come. I shouldn't have—" I collected myself. "Ray, he's so beautiful. He looks just like you."

Ray smiled. His little boy's name was Scotty. He was turning five in a month. His favorite sport was soccer. Kerry owned a bakery in town. Her parents lived close by. Things were good. "That's good," I said. That's really good." And I meant it, Dan. It was really, really good. Somehow Ray survived. And I found some weird sense of salvation in that.

"Are you sure you don't want to come in for coffee?"

I could see Ray's house from where we were sitting. There were things about it I hadn't noticed earlier. The pretty flower boxes under the windows. The tire swing. I wiped away the tears that were beginning to fill my eyes. "No, I think I better go."

Ray walked me to my car. We stood there for a moment without speaking.

"You know," I said, "for a while after Daniel died I'd go to my room, pull down the shades, turn on the record player, close my eyes, and pretend that he and I were hanging out on his bed listening to music, and I'd talk to him. I'd repeat conversations as best I could and after a while I would open my eyes and adjust to the light and to the fact that he wasn't alive, but during that time—well, during that time no one could take him away."

I reached into my bag for the envelope and handed it to him. "Knowing you, you haven't changed the locks."

"I waited a long time, Suza."

"You did. I'm sorry."

I stepped into the car, closed the door. He tapped the window. I rolled it down.

"You know you can always close your eyes." I nodded my head.

"Friends?"

"Friends would be nice."

And that's what we became.

Me, Kerry, Ray, and Scotty. We became friends.

The conductor ANNOUNCES OUR ARRIVAL: "FARMINGDALE." Three syllables. Farm-ing-dale. Heaving with strip malls, an amusement park, and dead people. The train slows. I button Mai's jacket. I don't want to be buried in Farm-ing-dale.

Ray is waiting for us at the bottom of the platform. He takes Mai from my arms, carries her to the car, buckles her in tight. A thin layer of frost coats the windshield. "You okay?" he asks before starting the car. I nod my head yes, then direct my focus to the leafless trees that flank the service road. Just behind them, tombstones puncture a flat gray sky. "Farmingdale." Three syllables. Farm-ing-dale. Heaving with strip malls, an amusement park, and dead people. Ray stops for a light. The Outdoor Saloon is having a sale on patio furniture. *2 days only.* The light turns green. I don't want to be buried in Farm-ing-dale.

Mai cranes her neck toward the window. I wonder what she sees. I wonder what she already knows of leafless trees, tombstones, rust-resistant chaise lounges.

Train. Taxi. Graveyard.
Ten. Eleven. Twelve.

It's New York City, 1983. Daniel's walking down a hill. He's heading toward the yard. What he's doing is against the law. He doesn't care. He's seeking justice. Justice has little to do with righteousness. People tell him otherwise. They must. They're people.

Daniel is walking along the rail. Ray is waiting for him at the foot of a sleeping subway car. What they're doing is against the law. They don't care. They review plans. Ray's utilizes color. Daniel's scale. Tonight they will exploit both. AJAX and JAKYL. Bright and Loud. Tourniquet and warning.

JAKYL throws up. AJAX fills in. The perpetrators, in navy and white, are golden. The victim brown. Bound like a pig. Restrained at the neck. The victim's eyeballs pop. "Michael's eyeballs are popping." When Daniel says his name, the piece becomes human.

One policeman brandishes a gun. The other a rope. Both smiles are in profile. If there were more time, AJAX and JAKYL would paint more detail. For now it must be by implication. Michael Stewart is—the letters shatter over his heart—D-E-A-D.

Krylon Cherry Red teardrops travel through a single beam of light. They look so real Daniel decides they're not paint. They're blood. Ray is spraying blood onto Michael Stewart's face. It's his blood. Daniel shakes his head. Focuses. There's no wind tonight. The starless sky is still. It's everyone's blood.

Ray puts down the can. They step back to admire the piece and the silence consents. There is no triumph in this. So when Ray says, "It is what it is, Dan," Daniel knows Ray's not talking about the work. All these years of running through subway tunnels, diving onto moving trains, leaping over live rails. All these years. Certain. If you're bold enough, people will hear you . . .

"Yeah," Daniel says, "it is what it is."

And then it happens. On the exhale. God teases like that, which is why Daniel doesn't believe in God.

A cop shouts, "Don't move."

Ray says, "Fuck."

Daniel says, "Jump."

Ray wavers.

"Go!"

But Ray doesn't move. Daniel thinks this is out of loyalty: "It's okay. I'll be right behind you."

Nothing.

He thinks it's out of fear: "You can make it."

Still nothing.

Daniel shoves Ray off the train. The cops willingly distort this as an act of aggression. Bullets are discharged. One hits a can of paint. The can explodes into a ball of fire. Ray lands unharmed. He stops. Looks back. Their eyes meet.

GO!

There is fire everywhere. Daniel sees it coming and begins to process that it will burn him. That he will have burned alive writing a love song. He starts to smile but remembers.

"Ray, get to Suza before the cops do." As he shouts this he's aware she is all he will miss. "Tell her that I love her." It doesn't matter who gets to her or when. The grief is total. Not believing in God costs him.

Flames rain down from a beckoning sky. It will be winter soon. Then spring. Daniel begins to spin, arms in air, palms toward sky, his body around in circles. He is scared but he feels no fear. He doesn't plead. He simply spins. An offering. He spins and spins. An act of faith. A shaggy-headed kid. A box of crayons. A lefty. He draws a circle. He colors it yellow. He applies two eyes, a nose, a smile. He spins and spins. The crayon becomes paint, the paper a subway car. He announces himself. Again in yellow: J-A-K-Y-L. He is the JAKYL. He spins. He's seventeen. He spins. He's alive. He spins. This matters. I AM ALIVE. He spins and spins. Nearly imperceptible now. He spins and spins until he's swallowed.

Whole.

The entrance TO "ROLLING HILLS" LOOKS LIKE THE ENtrance to a suburban country club. Fancy font on a shiny brass plaque. Brick pillars. Iron gate. A guard greets us: "How can I help you?"

Ray says, "We're here to visit plot 122. Seliger."

"One moment please." The guard makes his way to the security hut, a small wooden structure with a flickering light. Ray and I look at each other, then look away.

The guard, Bernie according to his nametag, returns with a guest pass and instructions: "Just leave this in the front window, believe it or not they'll tow you." He hands us a map of the cemetery. "And this here will make it much easier to find the deceased." He takes a red Sharpie and marks directions. "Take Delancey down. At the end of the street make a left onto Orchard. Then a right onto—"

"Reed."

"Oh, you know your way. Sorry, the computer doesn't show that you've visited recently."

"Yeah. It's been a long time. I don't think there were computers the last time we visited." Ray turns on the engine.

"Thanks again," he says, and we continue on. Down Delancey. A left onto Orchard. In the side mirror I see Mai smile at a hovering angel.

Ray pulls over. "Ready?"

"Yeah. I'm ready."

Ray gets out of the car, walks around front, and opens the door. He takes Mai out of the car seat. She wraps her tiny arms around his shoulders, mooring herself to his heart. A totem all too familiar.

It's time.

Ray passes Mai to me. She's not a baby but she's little, so I can hold her in my arms.

"You're not coming with us?"

"You don't need me."

"I do."

"Nah." He smiles. Kindness filling his eyes. "Not this time."

And now. I WALK THROUGH THE GRAVEYARD WITH MY DAUGH-ter. We are wearing matching, well-structured, black coats. My daughter, a little Asian girl with long, straight, black hair, has accessorized hers with a white angora hat and matching muff. My hat and gloves are black. We could be anyone. Any woman and child making their way through a stone garden on the way to visit a loved one.

We follow the path. Up ahead, three, four graves maybe, I see myself. There I am, a teenager sitting on a blan-ket. Legs crossed. A mint green wool cap pulled down over my forehead obscures my eyes. I am wearing Daniel's varsity jacket. I look so much younger that it's hard to recognize my-self, but it's my voice I hear.

"They got off today, Daniel. The cops that killed Michael Stewart. They walked out of jail and into the daylight and right now they are probably at home having dinner with their fam-ilies, celebrating at a bar with friends. And you're here."

I watch my younger self place Life Saver candies at the base of his tombstone. Roll by roll, letters begin to form.

J–in cherry red

I'm not going to be back for a while, Daniel. What I mean is, I'm here to say goodbye. I'm sorry, you know. I shouldn't cry and I'm sorry—it's one of the things I really don't like about myself—how often I cry—but I'm getting better. Maybe one day I won't cry at all.

A–in orange

It's just that I don't want you to think that I don't love you, because I do, Daniel, I love you so much. But every time I come here, instead of feeling closer to you, you feel further away. Like, I can hardly remember what holding your hand felt like. If your skin was calloused or soft, your palms sweaty or dry. Did you grip or clasp?

K–in lemon yellow

I do remember what it was like—the feeling—how I felt when I held your hand. To feel safe like that, you know. Remember that spot we used to sit at by the river? Remember how hard it was to get down there and how you'd always go first and then reach for my hand and help me down and we'd walk along those rocks as far as we could and then sit down and watch the boats pass?

Y–in lime green

One time, do you remember, when it started to rain and there was lightning and I was scared we'd get struck by the lightning? You told me as long as I was with you there was nothing to worry about and then you grabbed my hand and we ran home. Gosh, I think we never stopped. Not once.

L–in pineapple white

You know I always believed you. I believe still—funny, right, to look at you?—but I do. I still believe that when I'm with you I'm safe. Imagine, to feel that kind of safety again. Out there in the real world with walking, talking people.

JAKYL

I look at the Life Savers covering your grave and re-arrange a few. "The sky is getting dark, Dan. It's probably going to rain, which is funny because it makes sense, you know, that it will rain tonight. That I couldn't sleep here one last time even if I wanted to. I'll probably be back home watching the news with Mom or helping cook dinner, what-ever it is that keeps me in the room, and I'll think of you when I hear the rain. I'll think of you here. Still here. These pretty colors bleeding into each other until they are washed away.

"I'll want to come back, to check on you, to make sure you're okay, but I'm not going to. I told you that, right? How I'm here to say goodbye. *See you later, alligator.* How I'm not coming back?"

And I didn't.

Mai watches me carefully. I kneel, place one hand on your headstone to support myself. With the other I run my fingertips across the earth. Your left cheek to right shoulder. Your right shoulder to heart. And Mai, because the language of grief knows no barrier, stands just behind me, so close I can feel her breath.

It begins to snow. The little girl has never seen snow before. In books and on television but never in real life— never *real* snow. Mai takes her hands out of her muff and waves them through the air; she opens her mouth, sticks out her tongue.

I experience my daughter's joy with the knowledge that there is a legacy to this kind of happiness. It will be woven into dialogue, used as both question and answer, reenacted in the parallel blackness that resides behind closed eyes.

Space and time will compress, are already compressing, and just as snowflakes don't exist in duplicate, no two memories can be the same. I will remember this moment years from now. My daughter as a little girl. I will remember her innocence. Her wonderment. The rosiness to her cheeks. The slight run in her tights.

And she will remember me. Remember the kindness in my eyes, the gentle sound of my voice. Or perhaps she won't reflect upon me at all. Perhaps she will associate this moment with the smell of roasted chestnuts. The dinging sound of a Salvation Army bell. Her first Christmas in New York City. Or, and this is most likely the case, she won't remember the specifics at all.

The only absolute is that this will be a moment we will each yearn for. A moment when the world felt at peace and hope, while irrational, somehow, in the middle of a graveyard, seemed perfectly possible.

We spent the night before you died by the river. It had been a long time since we hung out down there, but it was a nice night, so I didn't think anything of it. You climbed under the barrier, then took my hand and helped me through.

"Remember how we'd come down here to catch fireflies?" you asked.

"Of course I do. We'd bring them home to show Mom and Dad and then Dad would open the window and you and I would watch them twinkle away."

"Yeah. We haven't been down here much since Dad died. I'm sorry about that. You love it down here."

"Don't worry about it. We can come back again. We can come back tomorrow night if we want to."

It took you a second to respond and I hated myself for a long time, for not sensing the doubtfulness in your voice. "Yeah. Sure. Tomorrow night."

We settled into our spot, you lit a joint, and we hung out like that for a while. Listening to *Murmur*, gazing at the flat, glassy, black water.

"There's one night Suze that I remember in particular because you asked me how they glowed. You were kind of obsessed with it and I had no idea but I didn't want to let you down, so I said—"

"You said, 'Every firefly has a light bulb in its tail.'"

"You remember that?"

"Yep. And then I asked you how God goes about changing the bulb when it blows and you even had an answer for that: 'They come with a lifetime warranty. As long as a firefly lives it glows.'"

"I was a good big brother."

"The best big brother."

You got up then and began to spin. Arms in air. Palms toward sky. Like I'd seen you do countless times. Around and around.

"You know they're poisonous, fireflies. Whatever makes them glow is toxic. Did you know that?"

"No." I must have sensed something was off, because I giggled. I didn't know this about myself back then, but I giggle like that when I'm nervous.

"It was in the paper this morning. Some kid in Long Island ate a bunch of them and died."

"Why would anyone eat a firefly?"

You gestured for the joint, took a hit. "For the chance to glow, I guess."

The song ended and a new song came on. A really pretty song. You reached for my hand. "Spin with me."

"I'm too high. I'll fall."

"Nah," you said as you pulled me up. "I won't let you fall."

It was the sixth song. I know that because I listened to that album again and again for many years. Hoping to feel you holding me like you did that night, as we spun.

"A firefly can't live without its light."

"Oh my gosh, you're so stoned."

"It's just kinda amazing. To think the thing that kills one thing is the same thing that keeps it alive."

I went along with the firefly conversation because you were always the most fun to get high with. The theories conjured. You would play them up for your audience. Imitate, mock gestures, gesticulate with your hands. But the best was the way you laughed when you were high. Sweet and easy. In gratitude almost.

Your laugh would make me laugh. Because you were funny, sure. But also because you were joyful. And that's all I ever wanted for you, Dan. For you to experience joy. Unburdened and free. Is that what they meant to you, the drugs? Mushrooms, journey? Acid, flight?

"So you're saying that if some firefly hunter found a firefly and stole its light, the firefly would die?"

"Well, not immediately. First it would lose its ability to fly, then to walk. The point is you take away a firefly's light and it dies just like any other bug."

"That's sad."

You stopped spinning, put your hands on my shoulders, and looked at me all serious.

"That's what I thought when I read about it in the paper this morning, but you know what, Suze? It's not sad. Because no one can take that away from him, even if for only a moment. Even if he can no longer glow. He once glowed."

Later that night I snuck into your room with my blanket and pillow and planted myself on the floor next to your bed. I listened to your breath. Heavy and even. In then out. I remember being very aware at that moment that I had a brother, he was alive, and I was safe.

"Daniel?" I said into the dark.

"Yeah?"

"I won't let anyone take my light."

"It's not always up to you," you said.

In eighth grade my science teacher, Mr. Simmons, taught our class about the speed of light and its relationship to time. He explained that when you're in a room and someone turns off the light, there's a split second between when that light goes out and when you see it go out. Then he explained that there's a split second of a split second between when the retinas in our eyes see it go out and when our brain processes what we saw. It was all very confusing but what I took home from class was that no matter how infinitesimally small it is, there is a measure of time between when something happens and when you realize it happened. What I didn't understand until after everything happened is that your light had already been stolen. I just didn't realize it was gone.

"Mommy." Mai pulls at my hand. "Mommy, dis?" She opens her mouth and catches a snowflake on the tip of her tongue. Then she gestures her chin toward the sky, asking me to join her. I, tears clearly in my eyes, hesitate. It's almost too much.

Everything you love gets taken away.

But look at us. Mother and daughter. Arms locked. Tongues outstretched. Capturing magic.

Everything.

I want to thank singer-songwriter Slaid Cleaves. I would not have been able to complete this book without the song "Cry" from his album *Everything You Love Gets Taken Away*.